"Stephen Vizinczey's name is difficult to spell or pronounce but it is worth learning, because he is a master of our time," wrote the leading Spanish weekly *Epoca* last year, commenting on the Spanish edition of *An Innocent Millionaire*. It is safe to say that there is no other English-language novelist writing about America who is so widely read and praised around the world and at the same time so little known in the United States.

Born in Hungary in 1933, Vizinczey was a young poet and playwright in his student days: three of his plays were banned by the Communist regime. His father, a Catholic antifascist teacher, was assassinated by the Nazis; under the Communists one of his uncles was beaten to death as he was being persuaded to sign away his land to the collective. Such formative experiences may account for some of the violent turns in Vizinczey's writing. After fighting in the defeated revolution of 1956, he escaped to the West, knowing about fifty words of English. Now he is described as a master of the language and praised for "teaching the English how to write English" (Anthony Burgess). After living in Montreal, Toronto, New York, and then Anna Maria Island, he eventually settled in London. "Having learned to write well in his adopted tongue," wrote the Los Angeles critic Bruce Bebb, "it would have been easy for him to shape a career as a Communist-baiter, one of those pathetic sycophants who pretend to see only evil on the east side of the Iron Curtain and only good in the West. Instead he chose to kick against the pricks wherever he went." Though Vizinczey's books were banned in Communist countries, it is true that he never conformed to the anti-Communist stereotype of the Cold War period. His chief inspiration as a novelist comes from a young European's sudden shock and amazement at finding himself in North America. Both *In Praise of Older Women* and *An Innocent Millionaire* portray our continent in the light of a European childhood; they reflect America through European eyes.

They have not found favor with America's literary establishment. The title of *In Praise of Older Women* has entered the language, but when the novel was first published in 1966 it was so little noticed in New York that it had to be remaindered after three months. Nevertheless, it has survived the changing attitudes and tastes of more than two decades. Just in 1990 it has been published in new Swedish, German, and Portuguese translations, and the Spanish translation has gone through fourteen printings in the last two years alone. Few novels praised by our literary journals and touted by the mass media have shown such widespread and enduring appeal. The Hungarian translation, finally published in Vizinczey's native land in 1990, appeared in a first edition of 100,000 copies. The present University of Chicago Press edition is the forty-first in English.

Vizinczey's attack on leading New York critics in his "Anatomy of Serious Rubbish, or The Bay of Pigs of the American Literary Establishment," published in *The Rules of Chaos* (1970), gained him no friends in the media, nor did his portrayal of New York in *An Innocent Millionaire*, which was rejected by every New York publisher before its success in England. Though it was eventually published in New York, it remained for foreign critics to point out that *"An Innocent Millionaire* shows all the worms in the Big Apple"* (Antonio Deblas) and "Vizinczey's New York attorneys make Balzac's shyster lawyers look like little orphan boys" (Martin Halter). The *New York Times Book Review*, while praising Vizinczey's "vividly epigrammatic prose" and calling the novel "a rare accomplishment, a contemporary adventure told with style, wit and wisdom," gave it only a brief notice, and didn't mention that *An Innocent Millionaire* had anything to do with New York. Most leading publications, including the daily *New York Times*, have never reviewed it.

Critics in the rest of the country, less bound to literary fashion and politics and to seasonal trends in publishing, have always been kinder to Vizinczey's books. Back in 1966, when *In Praise of Older Women* was being ignored by all the authoritative journals, young Larry McMurtry, reviewing it for the *Houston Post*, called it "a pleasure, a brilliant first novel" and found that "Mr. Vizinczey writes of women beautifully, with sympathy, tact and delight, and he writes about sex with more lucidity and grace than most writers ever acquire." As for *An Innocent Millionaire*, many reviewers across the United States greeted it with as much enthusiasm as critics in Britain, Canada, Latin America, and Europe, likening it to the great nineteenth-century classics.

We hope that these editions of Vizinczey's novels and his collection of essays and reviews, *Truth and Lies in Literature*, will give many American readers the joy of discovery.

—Morris Philipson
Director, The University of Chicago Press

From the Reviews

"Stephen Vizinczey's *In Praise of Older Women* is in a fair way to driving us reviewers out of what is left of our minds. Here is this Hungarian rebel who in 1957 could scarcely speak a word of our language and who even today speaks it with an impenetrable accent and whose name moreover we can't pronounce, and he has the gall to place himself, with his first book and in his thirty-third year, among the masters of plain English prose. . . . When I was a boy, one of my schoolmasters gave me *Romeo and Juliet* to read. 'You'll fall in love one of these days,' he said to me, 'and you might as well learn to do it properly.' For the same reason I gave my copy of *In Praise of Older Women* to my sixteen-year-old son."
—Kildare Dobbs, *Saturday Night* (Toronto, 1965)

"Written with great lucidity and charm. . . . An astonishing number of overtones."
—Northrop Frye (1965)

"A rarity—an erotic novel in which sexual experience is not a torment, a novel which affirms its pleasures and joys in a style that the author keeps from ever getting inflated."
—Max Lerner, *New York Post* (1966)

"A funny novel about sex, or rather (which is rarer), a novel which is funny—as well as touching—about sex. . . . Elegant, exact, and melodious—has style and presence and individuality."
—Isabel Quigly, *Sunday Telegraph* (London, 1966)

"The author writes about one of the most tragic periods of European history in which women appear as the sole refuge, man's great consolation, the healers of wounds."
—Naim Kattan, *Liberté* (Montreal, 1966)

"A classically refined narrative, simmering with paradox and humor. An elegant entertainment, conjured out of our present chaos."
—Michael Ratcliffe, *The Times* (London, 1968)

"Like James Joyce, who was as far from being a writer of erotica as Dostoevsky, Vizinczey has a refreshing message to deliver: life is not about sex, sex is about life."
—John Podhoretz, *Washington Times* (1986)

"It tells a unique story, tender, pleasant and entertaining, which conquers the reader. A delicious book, as heady as a goblet of Tokay."
—Jorge Amado (1987)

"Erotic situations, games, frustrations, naive miscalculations, humiliations, joyful and tearful pleasures. . . . Vizinczey never exaggerates, he writes with clear detachment not devoid of irony: his graceful and suggestive style frees us from the anguish that love often brings with it. . . . A little masterpiece in which sex is knowledge and good literature."
—Maria Dols, *Ajoblanco* (Barcelona, 1988)

"From the very beginning, *In Praise of Older Women* seemed to belong among the classics."
—Günter Fischer, *Münchner Stadtzeitung* (Munich, 1988)

"An erotic classic of subtle complexity, humor, and wit. An invitation to the experience of love, to adventure. But it is also the portrait of someone who is familiar to us from family stories, someone we have all known at some time. And perhaps his great success is owing to this, and to his style, which is so unaffected, so natural and at the same time so perfectly exact."
—Menene Gras Balaguer, *La Vanguardia* (Barcelona, 1988)

"Eroticism with profundity and wit. . . . Vizinczey's prose is crystal-clear and gracefully poignant and one reads the novel with a sensation of continuous hormonal delight."
—Jorge Lech, *Diario 16* (Madrid, 1989)

"It settles accounts with the political and social past of Hungary under the Soviets and it gives us critical glimpses of life in Italy, Canada and the United States as well. . . . deserves to be read and re-read—and then re-read again."
—Juan Domingo Argüelles, *Universal* (Mexico City, 1990)

STEPHEN VIZINCZEY

In Praise of Older Women

the amorous recollections of András Vajda

REVISED EDITION

THE UNIVERSITY OF CHICAGO PRESS

'This book is addressed to young men
and dedicated to older women—
and the connection between the two is my proposition.'

The University of Chicago Press, Chicago 60637
© 1965, 1967, 1978, 1985, 1986 by Stephen Vizinczey.
All rights reserved. University of Chicago Press edition published 1990.
Printed in the United States of America.
99 98 97 96 95 94 93 92 91 90   6 5 4 3 2 1

Reproduced from the Atlantic Monthly Press edition 1985.

Library of Congress Cataloging-in-Publication Data

Vizinczey, Stephen, 1933–
    In praise of older women : the amorous recollections of András Vajda /
    Stephen Vizinczey. — Rev. ed.
        p.   cm.
    ISBN 0-226-85886-3 (pbk.)
    I. Title.
PR6072.I9137 1990
823'.914—dc20   90-40605
                                                                  CIP

Contents

Woher dein Recht, in jeglichem Kostüme,
In jeder Maske wahr zu sein? — Ich rühme.
                        — Rainer Maria Rilke

To Young Men Without Lovers

In all your amours you should prefer old women to young ones . . . because they have greater knowledge of the world.
Benjamin Franklin

This book is addressed to young men and dedicated to older women – and the connection between the two is my proposition. I'm not an expert on sex, but I was a good student of the women I loved, and I'll try to recall those happy and unhappy experiences which, I believe, made a man out of me.

I spent my first twenty-three years in Hungary, Austria and Italy and my adventures in growing up differed considerably from the adventures of young men in the New World. Their dreams and opportunities are influenced by dissimilar amorous conventions. I am a European, they are Americans; and what makes for an even greater difference, they are young today, I was young a long time ago. Everything has changed, even the guiding myths. Modern culture – American culture – glorifies the young; on the lost continent of old Europe it was the affair of the young man and his older mistress that had the glamour of perfection. Today young men believe in girls of their own age, convinced that they alone have anything worthwhile to offer; we tended to value continuity and tradition and sought to enrich ourselves with the wisdom and sensibility of the past.

And sex was only part of it. We came from large families and were used to getting along with people older than ourselves. When I was a small boy my grandparents, who lived on a farm near Lake Balaton, used to give a lunch party every summer attended by more than two hundred relatives.

I remember marvelling how many of us there were, sitting on long benches at long tables in the courtyard, between the house and the plum trees – rows and rows of aunts and uncles, cousins, in-laws, ranging from children to octogenarians. Members of such tribes knew no age barriers. We lived within a hundred miles of each other and we all loved the same songs.

The storm of war swept that courtyard clear. The Vajdas, once so close, now live on four continents. We are losing touch, like everybody else. America wasn't devastated by foreign armies, but the leafy courtyards are gone just the same. They were paved over for runways. Families fly apart, and each generation seems to belong to a different period of history. The big houses with room for grandparents, aunts and uncles are replaced by teenage hangouts, retirement homes and the quiet apartments of the middle-aged. Opportunities for young men to mingle with older women have greatly diminished. They don't have much faith in each other.

As I was lucky enough to grow up in what was still an integrated society, I have the extravagant notion that my recollections may bring about a better understanding of the truth that men and women have a great deal in common even if they were born years apart – and may thereby stimulate a broader intercourse between the generations.

As I'm going to describe my own experiences, I ought to reassure the reader that I don't intend to overwhelm him with my personal history. It is his curiosity about himself that I hope to stimulate. What follows is a highly selective memoir centred not so much on the personality of the narrator as on the universal predicaments of love. Still, to the extent that this book *is* an autobiography, I am conscious, like Thurber, of Benvenuto Cellini's stern dictum that a man should be at least forty years old and have accomplished something of excellence before setting down the story of his life. I don't fulfil either of these conditions. But, as Thurber says, 'Nowadays, nobody who has a typewriter pays any attention to the old master's quaint rules.'

András Vajda
Associate Professor
Department of Philosophy
The University of Michigan
Ann Arbor, Michigan

1 On Faith and Friendliness

Everything comes to us from others . . . To Be is to belong to someone.
Jean-Paul Sartre

I was born into a devout Roman Catholic family, and spent a great part of my first ten years among kindly Franciscan monks. My father was headmaster of a Catholic school and an accomplished church organist, an active and gifted young man who also had the energy and inclination to run the home guard in the district and participate in politics. Supporting the authoritarian pro-clerical regime of Admiral Horthy, he was the sort of conservative who was also an anti-fascist, and alarmed by Hitler's rise to power in Germany, he used his influence and authority to have the local meetings of the Hungarian Nazi Party banned. In 1935, when I was two years old, he was stabbed to death by an adolescent Nazi chosen for the task because he was not yet eighteen and couldn't be executed for the murder. After the funeral my mother fled from the horror of her loss to the nearest big town, the first, thousand-year-old city of Hungary, the name of which I won't torment you with. She rented an airy second-floor apartment on one of the main streets of the town – a narrow street of baroque churches and fashionable shops – just a few minutes' walk away from the Franciscan monastery, which I used to visit even before I reached school age. My father's services to the Church and his untimely death, and the fact that there were several priests on both sides of our family, endeared me to the fathers, and they always made me welcome. They taught me to read and write, they talked to me about the lives of the saints and the great heroes of Hungarian history, they told me about the far-off cities where they had studied – Rome,

Paris, Vienna – but above all they listened to whatever I wanted to say. So instead of having one father I grew up with a whole order of them; they always had a warm and understanding smile for me, and I used to walk in the wide, cool corridors of their monastery as if I owned the place. I remember their loving company as vividly as my own mother's, although, as I said, I lived alone with her from the age of two. She was a quiet and tender woman who always picked up things after me. Since I didn't play much with other children, I was never in a fight; and between the monks and my mother, I was surrounded with radiant love and a sense of absolute freedom. I don't think they ever tried to control me or bring me up, they just watched me grow, and the only restriction I felt was the awareness that they were all praying for me to do my best.

I was also very conscious of belonging to a large and splendid tribe, and was allowed to think of myself as the pride and joy of all my relations. I particularly recall one occasion when my uncles came with their families to visit their widowed sister on her birthday. There was a big to-do in the evening and I refused to go to sleep with the other children while the adults stayed up to have a good time. So they all came to my room to keep me company while my mother put me to bed. As she undressed me, she smacked my bottom and kissed it, and promised that they would all kiss it if I would go to sleep afterwards without any more fuss. I couldn't have been more than three or four at the time – this must be one of my earliest memories – and I still remember lying on my stomach and looking over my shoulder to see all those grownups lined up waiting their turn to kiss my bottom.

All this may account for the fact that I became an open-hearted and affectionate boy and a conceited brat. Taking it for granted that everyone would love me, I found it natural to love and admire everyone I met or heard about.

These happy emotions of mine were first directed to the

saints and martyrs of the Church. At the age of seven or eight I had the romantic determination to become a missionary and, if at all possible, a martyr, on the rice-fields of China. I remember particularly one sunny afternoon when I didn't feel like studying and stood at the window of my room watching the smartly dressed women walking back and forth along our street. I wondered whether, becoming a priest and taking a vow of celibacy, I would find it difficult to go through life without the company of those fluffy women who were walking by our house on their way to the hat-shop or the hairdresser to make themselves look even more angelic. My determination to become a priest thus confronted me with the problem of renouncing women even before I could possibly have wanted them. After feeling ashamed about my concern for some time, I finally asked my Father Confessor, a childlike, grey man in his sixties, how difficult *he* found it to go through life without women. He looked at me sternly and confined his answer to the remark that he didn't think I would ever be a priest. I was taken aback by his belittling of my determination – just because I had wanted to know the weight of the sacrifice – and was afraid he would like me less. But he brightened up again and told me with a smile (he was never short of encouragement) that there were many ways to serve God.

I used to serve as acolyte at his masses: an early riser, he liked to say mass at six o'clock, and often there was no one else in the huge cathedral but him and me, feeling the mysterious and powerful presence of God. And though I'm an atheist now, I can still recall and cherish that feeling of elation, the four candles in the cool marbled silence, filled with echoes. It was there that I learned to sense and love elusive mystery – an inclination that women are born with and men may acquire, if they are lucky.

I dwell upon these still-glittering fragments of memory partly because it's pleasant to think of them and partly, too, because I'm convinced that many boys ruin their best years –

and their characters – with the mistaken notion that one has to be a rough-tough kid to become a man. They join a football or hockey team to be grown-up, while in fact an empty church or a deserted country road would help them more to sense the world and themselves. The Franciscan fathers would, I hope, forgive me for saying that I would never have been able to understand and enjoy women as much as I do if the Church hadn't taught me to experience elation and awe.

To return to the question of celibacy as it begins to trouble a young Catholic boy, I must say that the women I saw from our apartment window weren't solely responsible for my premature anxiety. Just as I was able to participate in the lives of a group of men at the monastery, so at home I was often welcomed into a community of women. My mother used to give weekly tea-and-cookie parties for her friends, widows and single women of her own age, between thirty and forty. I remember that the similarity of the atmosphere at the monastery and at my mother's tea-and-cookie parties struck me as strange and wonderful. Both the Franciscans and my mother's friends were a happy and cheerful lot, apparently quite content to live on their own. I felt myself the only human link between these two self-contained worlds and I was proud that I was welcome and enjoyed myself in both. I couldn't imagine life without either of them and I sometimes still think that being a Franciscan monk with a harem of forty-year-old women would be the best way of living.

After a time I began to long for the afternoons when my mother's friends would come and take my head between their warm, soft hands and tell me what dark eyes I had: it was a dizzying joy to have them touch me or to touch them. I tried to imitate the martyrs' courage by jumping up to them when they arrived and greeting them with a kiss or a hug. Most of them looked surprised or bewildered on such occasions. 'Heavens, Erzsi, you have a nervous jumpy boy!'

they would say to my mother. A few of them suspected me, especially when I managed to have my hands fall on their breasts – for some reason this was more exciting than just touching their arms. However, these incidents always ended in laughter; I don't remember them being very intent on anything for very long. I loved them all, but I used to wait most eagerly for my father's sister, Aunt Alice, who was a slightly plump, big-breasted blonde, with an absolutely fantastic perfume and a round, beautiful face. She used to pick me up and look into my eyes with mock anger and some coquettishness, I believe, admonishing me in a stern-soft voice: 'You're after my breasts, you devil!'

Aunt Alice was the only one who gave me my due as a personage of grave importance. Having become the first Hungarian Pope and suffered a martyr's death in my imagination, I already viewed myself as a great saint, temporarily stranded in childhood. And though Aunt Alice attributed to me a different kind of greatness when she called me a devil, I felt that deep down we meant the same thing.

To free my mother from my company now and then, her friends used to take me for long walks or to the occasional movie. It was only my aunt, however, who broke the news of our going by asking me for a date. 'My handsome beau,' she would say with happy anticipation, 'will you take me to the theatre?' I remember particularly one day when I was going out with her in my first pair of long trousers. It was a sunny Saturday afternoon in the late spring or early fall – some time before the United States entered the war, for we were going to see *The Wizard of Oz*. I had got my adult suit a few days before and was anxious to show it off to Aunt Alice, who was sure to appreciate it. When she finally arrived, in the midst of her perfume and powder, she got so involved in explaining to my mother why she was late that she didn't notice my new trousers. However, as we were about to leave, she gave forth a throaty 'Aaaaahh!' and stepped back to gobble me up with her eyes. I held out my arm for her and as she took it she said: *'I've* got the handsomest escort today. Doesn't he look like his father, Erzsi?' We were walking towards the door, arm in arm, a happy couple, when suddenly I heard my mother's voice:

'András, did you remember to pee?'

I left the apartment with Aunt Alice, swearing to myself never to return. Even my blonde companion's soothing remarks sounded outrageously condescending, and as we walked down the stairs I wondered how I could re-establish the old equilibrium of our relationship. Just before we stepped out into the street, I pinched her bottom. She pretended not to notice, but blushed deeply. I decided then to marry Aunt Alice when I grew up, for she understood me.

However, I don't want to dramatize my boyhood by turning it into the story of my incestuous passion for that glorious lady. I was happiest with the Franciscan fathers and at my mother's weekly gatherings, when I saw all her friends together and could watch and listen to them chatting about fashion, the war, relatives, marriages and things I didn't understand. The vast and silent cathedral and our living room filled with all these cheerful, loud women, with the smell of their perfumes, with the light of their eyes – these are the strongest and most vivid images of my childhood.

I wonder, what kind of life would I have had if it hadn't been for my mother's tea-and-cookie parties? Perhaps it's because of them that I've never thought of women as my enemies, as territories I have to conquer, but always as allies and friends – which I believe is the reason why they were friendly to me in turn. I've never met those she-devils you hear about: they must be too busy with those men who look upon women as fortresses they have to attack, lay waste and leave in ruins.

Still on the subject of friendliness towards all – and towards women in particular – I can't help concluding that my utterly complete happiness at my mother's weekly tea-and-cookie parties indicated an early and marked enthusiasm for the opposite sex. It's obvious that this enthusiasm had a great deal to do with my later luck with women. And although I hope this memoir will be instructive, I have to confess that it won't help you to make women more attracted to you than you are to them. If deep down you hate them, if you dream of humiliating them, if you enjoy ordering them around, then you are likely to be paid back in kind. They will want and love you just as much as you want and love them – and praise be to their generosity.

2 On War and Prostitution

Every newborn is a Messiah – it's a pity he'll turn out a common rascal.
Imre Madách

Up to the age of ten, I was allowed to forget that I'd been born the same year Hitler came to power. In war-torn Europe, our city appeared to me as a capital of fairyland: it was tiny and toy-like, yet ancient and majestic, much like some older sections of Salzburg. Here I lived, a happy young prince in the best of all possible worlds, surrounded by a numerous and protecting family: my mother, that quiet and pensive woman, following me with her serene eyes; my aunts, those loud, earthy yet elegant friends of hers; and the Franciscan monks, my benign fathers. I was allowed to grow up in a hothouse of love, and absorbed it into the cells of my body. But perhaps it's just as well that, after learning to love the world, I also came to know it. From a happy-go-lucky boy toying with the idea of priesthood and blissful martyrdom, I turned into a pimp and a black-marketeer. At the end of the war – after two nightmarish years and before reaching the age of twelve – I became a go-between in charge of Hungarian prostitutes in an American Army camp near Salzburg, the city which in other respects was so much like my own.

My transformation began in the summer of 1943, when the waves of the war finally reached western Hungary. Our quiet city became a German garrison, and during the nights American bombers began to create new rubble beside the ancient ruins. Our apartment was requisitioned for the officers of the Wehrmacht, and none too soon either: a couple of weeks after we moved out, the house took a direct hit. To escape the air raids, we moved farther west to my grandparents' home in an out-of-the-way village, and in the fall my mother sent me to a military school in a small town near the Austrian border. She said I would be safe and properly fed there, and would be taught Latin.

The colonel who commanded the school summed up its spirit in his welcoming speech to the new first-year cadets: 'Here you will learn what discipline really means!' We were bellowed at every moment of the day, in the classroom, the courtyard and the dormitory. Every afternoon from three to four we had to walk up and down the park, which was large and heavily wooded and surrounded by high walls. We were ordered, on pain of severe corporal punishment, to walk briskly and never to stop for a second, and there were sergeants watching us – leaning against the trees – to make sure that we obeyed the rule. However, we junior cadets also had to obey the commands of senior cadets, who had some duly constituted military authority over us. I found myself in a quandary the very first day when a senior cadet walking behind me began to shout at me to stop and stand to attention. He was a thin, red-haired boy with a brush-cut, sickly and unimposing in appearance – in fact he looked younger than I did. I was worried about disobeying him, but even more worried about disobeying the sergeants. I walked on briskly and he had to run to catch up with me. By the time he reached my side he was sweating and out of breath. 'Salute me!' he demanded in a reedy and shaking voice. 'Salute me!' I saluted him and walked on, overcome by a feeling of revulsion. I was convinced I had been thrown among a bunch of raving idiots.

It was a shock from which I have never fully recovered. My one and a half years of drilling at the Royal Hungarian Officers' Training College very nearly turned me into an anarchist. I can neither respect nor trust senior cadets, generals, party leaders, millionaires, executives, nor any of their enterprises. Incidentally, this attitude seems to fascinate most women – perhaps because they are less overwhelmed than most men by the perfection of the man-made order of the world.

The senior cadets were especially concerned about the way we made our beds.

'Your bed must be as straight and smooth as glass!' our room commander would scream, throwing my blankets and sheets into the four corners of the dormitory. 'You need some practice!'

Even after the Russian armies entered Hungary and Admiral Horthy announced that further resistance was useless, that the greater part of the Hungarian Army, more than a million men, more than ten per cent of our population, had been killed, and that there could never be a Hungarian Army again – even then, the room commander was still obsessed by the smoothness of our blankets. When he threw apart my bed I had to remake it within three minutes; if it took me longer, as it always did, he threw the bed apart once again, and repeated the performance until he got bored with it. We played this bed game until the Russian troops reached the outskirts of the town. Then the colonel fled with his family and all his belongings in the trucks that had been designated for the evacuation of the cadets, most of the other officers disappeared, and we were led by a major, our history teacher, on a westward march through Austria. I wasn't to see a bed of any kind for several months.

About four hundred of us joined the chaotic mob of refugees who, fleeing from the war, remained in its constantly moving centre, right between the German and Russian armies. Marching between the front lines through the plains and mountains of Austria, we learned to sleep while walking, to walk past mutilated bodies, dead or still twitching, and I learned at last that the Cross stands not only for sacrifice and forgiveness but also for crucifixion. Being eleven and a half years old at the time, I was impressed for life by man's insane cruelty and by the fragility of our bodies. A religious upbringing is said to implant in one a sense of guilt about sex, but ever since those weeks of shock, hunger and exhaustion, the only forms of self-indulgence I recoil from are hatred and violence. It was then that I must have acquired the sensibilities of a libertine: when one sees too many corpses one is likely to lose one's inhibitions about living bodies.

Going through blacked-out Vienna in the middle of the night, I lost the other cadets, and from then on I was on my own. I lived on what I could steal from the fields by the road. Other refugees before me must have done the same, for the peasants were guarding their *kartoffel* patches with machine-guns, and I often got my skin burned before I could bake a potato. By the middle of May, 1945, when an American Army jeep picked me up on the road, alone and half-starved, I was ready for anything.

In saying that I became a whoremaster for the American Army before I reached my twelfth birthday, I don't mean to create the impression that the soldiers treated me unfeeling-ly or without any consideration for my youth. I certainly had a far better time in the US Army than at the military school. And if I did jobs inappropriate to my age, it was because I was anxious to earn my keep – and perhaps even more anxious to learn about sex. The two soldiers who picked me up brought me to the camp and saw to it that I was fed, showered, given a medical examination, and taken to the commanding officer. The doctor's report on my rundown physical condition and the visible effects of my nightmarish experiences must have aroused his pity, and he decided that I should stay in the camp. I was given a bed in one of the long brick barracks (built originally for the Hitler Youth), a cut-down uniform, a GI's ration of cigarettes, chewing gum and life-savers, and a canteen; and I lined up with the soldiers for the five-course dinner with a profound sense of well-being. For the next few days I spent most of my time wandering through the barracks, trying to make friends with the soldiers. They had little to do but look at pictures, shave, clean their clothes and guns, and teach a stray kid English words, 'Hi', 'OK', 'kid' and 'fucking' (as a universal adjective) were the first words I learned, in about that order; but within a couple of weeks I had picked up enough of the language to discuss the war, Hungary, the US and our families at home. One night I happened to be around when a Hungarian girl and a soldier were arguing about the price, and I volunteered my services as interpreter and mediator. Five packs of cigarettes, a can of powdered milk, twenty-four packages of chewing gum and a small can of beef were the main items of exchange. It turned out that most of the women who visited the camp by night, while the MPs looked the other way, were Hungarians from the nearby refugee camp; so I was soon active as a translator, go-between and procurer.

The first thing I learned in this adventurous occupation was that most moralizing about sex had absolutely no roots in reality. It was a revelation which came also to those surprised, respectable, sometimes even snobbish middle-class women whom I guided to the Army barracks from the crowded and destitute Hungarian camp. At the war's end, when even the Austrian inhabitants were in dire need of almost everything, the hundreds of thousands of refugees were hardly able to survive – and their position was all the more pitiful as most of them were used to a comfortable bourgeois style of living. Pride and virtue, which had been so important to these women in their own setting, had no meaning in the refugee camp. They would ask me – blushing, but often in front of their silent husbands and children – whether the soldiers had venereal disease and what they had to offer.

I fondly recall one beautiful and high-born lady who was extravagantly dignified about the whole business. She was a tall dark woman, with huge vibrating breasts, and a bony face glowing with pride – in her early forties, I would guess. Her husband was a count, the head of one of the oldest and most distinguished families in Hungary. His name and his military rank, even though it belonged to Admiral Horthy's beaten army, were still potent enough to secure them a separate wooden shack among the refugees. They had a long-haired daughter about eighteen years old who used to giggle whenever I entered their place on my not too frequent errands. Countess S. would only go with an officer, and only for two or three times the usual rate. The Count used to turn his head away when he saw me. He still wore the trousers of his dress uniform, black with broad gold stripes down the side; but above them, instead of the coat with its gold-fringed epaulettes, he wore a disintegrating old pull-over. I had an eerie feeling in his presence, remembering the pages about his family in our elementary school history books, and the pictures of him, the great general reviewing his troops, in the newspapers we'd been given to read at the cadet school. He rarely returned my greeting, while his wife always received me like an unpleasant surprise – as if she herself hadn't asked me to report to her whenever I had any requests from *nice clean officers* who were *not too demanding*.

'It's that boy again!' she used to cry, in a pained, exasperated voice. Then she would turn to her husband with a dramatic gesture. 'Do we absolutely need anything today? Can't I tell this immoral boy to go to hell, just for once? Do we really need anything so badly?' As a rule the general didn't answer, just shrugged his shoulders listlessly; but he occasionally snapped back: 'You're the one who does the cooking, you should know what we need.'

'If you had gone over to the Russians with your troops, I wouldn't have to defile myself and commit mortal sin to feed us!' she cried once, in a state of sudden hysteria.

Although I'm translating the dialogue, she did use these quaint, unreal expressions like 'defile', 'commit mortal sin', and 'immoral boy' (which I used to like). She had not only the vocabulary but the bearing of a formidably righteous lady, and I half-sympathized with her, sensing what she must have gone through before stooping to 'defile herself'. Yet I couldn't help finding her distress slightly exaggerated, especially since she repeated her scenes with such exactness that I had the impression she was acting in a play. Her ritual challenge to her husband was never picked up, but their daughter was curiously eager to relieve her mother and do some of the sacrificing for the family herself. 'Let *me* go, mother – you look tired,' she would say. But the Countess wouldn't hear of it.

'I'd rather starve!' she stated angrily. 'I'd rather see you dead than selling yourself!' And sometimes she added with despairing humour, 'I'm too old to be corrupted, it doesn't matter any more what I do.'

We all waited silently while she collected herself, put on her make-up, and then stood watching her husband or just looking around the little room. 'Pray for me while I'm gone,' she usually said as we walked out, and I followed her almost convinced that she would be glad to die if only she could avoid the coming ordeal.

By the time we reached the car, however, she could manage a brave smile, and on occasions when a certain young captain was waiting for her, she used to laugh happily and quite freely on our way to the Army camp. And when her face suddenly grew dark and pensive, I felt as if I would catch fire just sitting beside her. At such times one could see that she had the most sensuous mouth. I often observed similar changes of mood in the women I escorted to the barracks; they departed from their families as goddesses of virtue who were being sacrificed, and then quite unmistakably enjoyed themselves with the Americans, who were often younger and handsomer than their husbands. I suspected that many of them were quite glad to be able to think of themselves as noble, unselfish and self-sacrificing wives and mothers while in fact taking a welcome holiday from marital boredom.

Not that I was ever present while they were actually with

the soldiers in the barracks, although I made many futile attempts to stay around. After all, I wasn't receiving any pay for my services, and I somehow felt the soldiers and the women owed me the chance to pick up some firsthand knowledge of their activities. But no matter how casual they were about the harmful impressions I might be subjected to in arranging their meetings, they drew the line at the start of their lovemaking, and wouldn't allow me to stay and watch. Sometimes when I grew too excited by some preliminary necking that took place in front of me, I used to protest against the injustice of it all. 'I'm not a kid when you need me to fix you up, but I'm a kid when it comes to fucking!' I wanted my ration of that too. I was so busy translating phrases like 'Ask her whether she's tight or wide,' I was so inflamed by all the talk and caresses, that I was in a state of permanent erection.

I rarely missed a chance to slip into an officer's hut after he had left it with a woman. In the soldiers' barracks there was always someone else around, but in an officer's private quarters I could sometimes examine the scene undisturbed. I tried to pick up clues from the rumpled beds, the half-empty liquor bottles, the lipstick-smeared cigarette butts – but most of all from the smells still lingering in the room. Once I even found a pair of white silk panties, and sniffed them greedily. They had a peculiar but pleasant odour. I had no way of knowing, but I was sure that the smell must be from the female stuff, and I pressed the panties to my nostrils and breathed through them for a long while.

I remember only one occasion when I actually felt I might as well stay a kid a bit longer. I was watching a soldier who had caught venereal disease and had just been given several injections right into the penis. While the other soldiers sat around in the barracks laughing their heads off, he walked up and down between the two rows of beds, still bent over with pain and keeping his hands between his legs. His eyes were filled with tears and he was shouting in a hollow voice:

'I'll never screw anyone but my wife! That's the last hooker I'll screw as long as I live!'

It was several days before I began again to consider how I could arrange to make love with one of the ladies I served.

My thoughts centred around Countess S. Although she called me 'that immoral boy', I couldn't help feeling that she must like me at least better than one of our lieutenants – a fat southerner with false teeth – whom she used to visit sometimes. While I couldn't hope to compete with the good-looking young captain, I thought I might get through to her after a night with the lieutenant. One morning I saw him drive away and hung around his quarters until she got up. When I heard her turn on the shower I slipped in. She didn't hear me enter the room and, opening the bathroom door stealthily, I could see her under the shower, heart-stopping, naked. Although I had seen a great many pin-up pictures on the walls of the barracks, this was the first time I saw a woman naked in the flesh. It was not only different, it was miraculous.

She didn't notice me, and when she stepped out of the shower I took her by surprise, kissed her breasts and pressed myself against her wet, warm body. Touching her, I was overcome with a happy weakness, and though I wanted to look at her I had to close my eyes. It was perhaps because she couldn't help noticing the deep impression her body made on me, that she waited a few moments before pushing me back with revulsion. 'Get out of here,' she hissed, covering her nipples with her hands. 'Turn your back!'

I turned my back and offered to get her ten cans of powdered milk, five cartons of powdered eggs, and all the cans of meat she wanted, if only she would let me lie down with her. But she threatened to scream for help if I didn't leave her alone. Having my back to her and imagining her putting on clothes and covering herself, I got such painful cramps that I had to sit down on the lieutenant's bed. After she had dressed, she sat down beside me and turned my face towards her with a sharp gesture. She seemed depressed.

'How old are you?'

'I'm grown up.'

I thought of asking her to see for herself, but there was no need. Looking down at me, she shook her head in despair. 'God, what does the war do to all of us!'

For once, I had the feeling she really meant what she said.

'You're being corrupted and ruined here. You should go back home to your mother.'

I think she was depressed both by my degradation and her own, which had brought her to the point where a mere kid could make a pass at her.

'The lieutenant had to go to town and he won't be back for a long time. And I have actually better contacts in the kitchen than he has. The cooks like me. I can get you anything.'

'You shouldn't think of love as something you buy. And you should wait until you're older. Wait till you get married. Your wife will keep herself clean for her marriage and so should you.'

Sitting on the lieutenant's bed and hearing the GIs' voices outside, she herself must have sensed the irrelevance of her statement. We just sat there side by side, and she asked about my family and where I was from, while she waited for the officer to come back and pay her.

'So you walked all the way to Salzburg,' she said in a wondering tone, as if she wanted to understand the kind of kid I was. 'You had to grow up quickly,' she added rather absent-mindedly and with a tinge of sympathy. Maybe she was testing her feelings towards the possibility of anything happening between us. She turned her face away from me, but not before I caught its faint expression of humbleness and surprise. Even after being a part-time prostitute, she must have despaired to find herself considering the offer of a twelve-year-old boy. Or so I interpreted her reaction. But while I thought I understood her, I couldn't think of anything to say or do which would draw her to me. I wasn't prepared. I felt as I had in school when the teacher called me up in front of the class and I couldn't name the capital of Chile. I wanted to get away, I was scared.

But just at that moment she pushed me gently back on the bed and unzipped my trousers. She began to play with me with quiet, slow fingers, still sitting up straight and watching my face with a gleam of curiosity; then her lips suddenly parted, she leaned down and held me in her mouth.

I soon became weightless and felt like I never wanted to move again in my life. I was half-conscious of her serious eyes watching me, and later on I seemed to hear her voice calling me an immoral boy again. At last she shook me by the shoulder and told me to get up: she didn't want the lieutenant to find me there when he came back. As I left the hut she admonished me to pray to God to save me from ruin.

Perhaps I might have been able to wear her down if I had kept on pestering her at the shower doors of the various officers' quarters which she visited. Yet, curiously enough, I didn't try. Her impulsive gesture in delivering me from my misery on the lieutenant's bed discouraged me from trying to catch women off their guard. I felt like a thief who has broken into a house – only to be surprised by the owner and sent off with a gift.

3 On Pride and Being Thirteen

No, thank you!
Edmond Rostand

Back in the cadet school I had heard a lot about the dangers
of sex. At masturbation time, after the lights were turned out
in the dormitory, we used to scare each other with stories
about boys who turned into imbeciles because they played
with themselves or had intercourse with girls. I remember
one tale about a kid who cracked up just from thinking about
women. By the time I got to the American Army camp I had
lost all my religious fears, but I still believed that if a boy had
a very strong sex-drive, his other faculties would be stunted.
And I worried a great deal about myself.

In retrospect, I find that my appetites were evenly over-
developed. For one thing, I became a food addict. Probably
because I had been hungry for so long before the Americans
took me in, I spent hours every day eating. There was a big
mess hall, one side of which was taken up by the row of
kitchen helpers – between six and eight of them at each
mealtime – who filled our canteens from their steel cooking
pots as we passed by. The round, sunny pancakes with
butter and syrup, corn niblets, and ice-cream and apple pie
were my favourites. I also developed an insatiable appetite
for money. During my first month or so in the camp, I
watched with unceasing disbelief the cooks who poured into
garbage containers the fat in which they cooked the ham-
burgers and steaks. They must have thrown out about
twenty or thirty gallons of fat every day – gallons of flowing
gold in starving Europe. I loved the Americans but they were
obviously crazy. The day after my failure to seduce the
Countess, I decided I would be a businessman, and hit upon

the idea of asking the chief cook to give me the fat instead of letting it go to waste. At first he didn't want to bother, but when I told him I wanted to *sell* the stuff, he agreed. From that day on, whenever the soldiers were driving me into Salzburg to get them girls from the refugee camp, they were also transporting my five-gallon milk-powder cans filled with fat. I sold them to various Salzburg restaurateurs and insisted on getting paid in American money. On days when I had more fat than I could sell, I used to give it away to the refugees, and received ovations worthy of a Hungarian Pope. After a while the chief cook (who never asked me for a cut) really got into the spirit of the thing and gave me every five-gallon can of meat, egg-powder, fruit or juice that had been opened and might spoil. Picking up the riches in the kitchen took about twenty minutes a day, getting to and from Salzburg and distributing them took another couple of hours. With two and a half hours of work a day I was earning about five hundred dollars a week. When Colonel Whitmore, the commander of the camp, heard about my talent for free enterprise he became curious about me and often invited me over to chat. He was one of the most civilized people I ever met: a short, thin man with a pale face and a slight twitch in one eye. The GIs told me he had seen a lot of action in the Pacific and had been given this European assignment as a kind of holiday. He didn't drink or play poker, and his chief recreation was reading: he seemed to know as much about Greek literature and mythology as the Franciscan fathers, and liked to talk about the plays of Aeschylus and Sophocles. He owned several hotels in and around Chicago, and was anxious to get back home and put them in order, but he told me he was just as bored with business as with the Army. I used to tell him about my sharp dealings with the restaurateurs, which seemed to amuse him, and he made me give an account of how much money I earned each day. After he learned that I was losing hundreds of dollars at poker, he took my profits for safe keeping. He had two children whom he missed very much, and he seemed to like to have me around, talking about anything that came into my head. But when I began to tell stories about the soldiers in the barracks, he cut me short: 'Watch it! Don't turn into a stool-pigeon. I don't want to hear about it.' He often took me on his rounds, and I happened to be with him when he was looking over a German Army warehouse he had to dispose of. It was stuffed with summer shirts which had been manufactured for Rommel's African Army and then forgotten. There were two million of them, according to the inventory, and I asked the commander to give them to me. He didn't think much of my chance of selling two million summer shirts, but he promised to let me have them and even to arrange transportation if I could find a buyer. I got on a jeep going to Salzburg and decided to look up the madam of a whorehouse I knew. She offered a thousand dollars for the lot, but I worked it up to eighteen hundred. Unfortunately, after we delivered the shirts and I collected the cash, the GIs who had driven the trucks sat down to play poker with me. I lost fourteen hundred dollars before deciding to give up the game once and for all.

Anxious to improve myself, I found a music teacher in Salzburg who gave me piano lessons twice a week, for half a pound of butter an hour. I was studying German and trying to improve my English. Having given up my ambition to become a martyr, I was now dreaming about becoming a living immortal: I began to write a long verse play about the futility of existence, hoping that it would be both a masterpiece and a hit. But I worked hardest of all studying Latin. For some reason I was convinced that I would never amount to anything if I didn't know Latin.

During all this time, I remained a virgin pimp. There were a few nice-looking and friendly whores who seemed to be fond of me, but I didn't know how to proposition them for myself. Staring as pleadingly as I could, I hoped it would occur to one of them to ask *me*. But they never did. And although I wanted to make love so badly that I often had severe cramps, the gloomy after-effects of straight business deals were beginning to intimidate me. I noticed that the soldiers who took on whoever was available – hardly even looking at the woman – were frequently sullen or angry afterwards. And while my dear Countess used to part from the young captain in a mood of high elation, she came out of the other officers' quarters looking bleak. Whatever else sex was, it was obviously teamwork, and I began to suspect that strangers who were more or less forced on each other rarely made a good team.

The woman who spelled this lesson out for me was Fräulein Mozart. She appeared in our barracks one bright Sunday in early spring, just after lunch, when most of the soldiers had already gone out for the afternoon. There were only three of us inside, two GIs and myself: one of them was sprawled on his bed reading magazines, and the other was giving himself a shave with some difficulty. He had put the mirror on the window-sill beside his bed, and the sun was getting in his eyes. I sat cross-legged on my bed, studying Latin verbs. Suddenly the door sprang open and our self-styled comedian from Brooklyn bellowed cheerfully into the room: 'Here she is, boys – Fräulein Mozart!'

Our barracks were long and narrow, with twenty-four beds on each side and a space of six feet or so between the two rows. My bed was towards the far end of the room, and when the newcomers entered I was able to slip to the very back without being noticed. I sat down on the floor behind the last bed, with only the top of my head showing, and hoped the others would forget about me so I could watch. Fräulein Mozart was a big Austrian blonde. Milky, massive, stolid. She wore a dirndl skirt with flowers on it and a sleeveless black blouse. She walked in as if there was nobody in the room; and, indeed, the two soldiers near the door did not greet her nor even seem to notice her entrance, though her escort made quite a scene. He was a short man with thick, dark eyebrows and close-cropped hair, and he was swinging his hips and clapping and rubbing his hands as he repeated his victory cry: 'How about *that*, guys – Fräulein Mozart!' He followed along behind her, making broad circling motions with his hands in the air to emphasize her contours. But his comrades paid no attention: the GI behind *Life* magazine didn't look up at all, and the other turned his lathered cheek from the mirror only for a second, then back again, squinting into the sun.

'The best piece you've ever seen!' Brooklyn insisted, unzipping his trousers with a flourish.

Fräulein Mozart slowed down, hesitated. I thought she found the presence of the others and her escort's behaviour embarrassing. Then she spoke, in a manner that showed me I had been mistaken.

'Which is your bed?' she asked brusquely.

Brooklyn pointed it out to her: it was towards the middle of the room, ten beds or so away from me. As casually as if she were alone, Fräulein Mozart began to undress, tossing her blouse and brassiere on the bed next to Brooklyn's. He stopped swinging and clapping his hands and just stared at her. Then she took off her skirt and unfastened her long blonde hair and began to comb it with her fingers. There she stood, naked but for her underpants, and all I could see was her broad white back and sturdy buttocks. I tried desperately to picture what Brooklyn was seeing from the front, as he sat on the edge of the next bed, very still now, tapping his foot softly. The other soldiers still didn't take any notice of her. This was utterly incomprehensible to me.

'If either of you guys are interested, I'm charging two pounds, ten dollars or four hundred cigarettes.'

She must have been visiting the British camp nearby and obviously didn't need me to translate. The soldiers didn't bother to answer. Just as she was tossing her panties in her partner's face, the reader of *Life* looked up to ask, 'Where's the kid?'

I ducked my head under the bed and held my breath, but then I heard Fräulein Mozart's flat, even voice: 'There's a kid down there at the back of the room.'

And her back had been turned to me all this time.

The men were still laughing as I walked out the door. I waited for her outside the barracks, kicking stones and hating the world. It was now or never, I was fed up. Fräulein Mozart emerged in about twenty minutes. Stepping up to her I realized that I only came up to her breasts, so I quickly stepped back again. I offered her a thousand cigarettes. She looked at me impassively and I thought she hadn't understood.

'I'll give you a thousand cigarettes.'

'What for?' she asked, slightly puzzled.

I decided to appeal to her in her native tongue. 'Fräulein, ich möchte mit Ihnen schlafen, wenn ich bitten darf.'

'Sure,' she answered, without any visible reaction. 'But I charge only four hundred cigarettes.'

I was pleased that she didn't want to overcharge me, even though I had offered the five cartons voluntarily. It gave me hope that we would be able to get along. I was sure of it when she herself suggested a place: the forest between the camp and the nearest village. Evidently Brooklyn had refused to drive her back to Salzburg and she had to go to the village to catch a bus into the city. I went back to the barracks to pick up the cigarettes and a blanket, walking slowly and casually because I didn't want the soldiers to ask any questions. Brooklyn was lying on his bed, naked, smoking and reading the comics. It took me about three minutes to collect my things, and I broke out in a sweat imagining that another GI had picked her up in the meantime, or that she had simply changed her mind and walked away. After all, she hadn't even smiled at me. But I was lucky: she was waiting.

We walked out of the camp through an opening in the wire fence. As peace and order were re-established, women were barred from the barracks; so while just as many women came to the camp as before, now they didn't pass through the gate.

It was one of the first clear, warm days of the year: the sun was dazzling and the earth, dark-wet from the melted snow, gave forth the smells of spring. The village of Niederalm was about a mile and a half away, and we didn't have far to go before reaching the forest. We were walking on a narrow side-road covered with pebbles. Fräulein Mozart was wearing flat-heeled shoes and walked with long easy strides, so that I had to trot to keep up with her. She never said a word or even looked towards me – it was as if she were walking alone, though she slowed down after a while. I thought of putting my hand on her bare white arm, but since I would have had to more or less reach up for it, I abandoned the idea. I looked to see if her breasts were shaking as she walked, but she wore a tight brassiere and they were as motionless as her face. However, they were large and round. I wanted her to know how much all this meant to me.

'Du bist die erste Frau in meinem Leben.'

'Ach so,' she answered.

After this exchange we marched on silently. The blanket was getting heavy and I was looking forward to spreading it on the ground. I was certain that once on the soft blanket beside me she would be kinder.

When we reached the forest – one of those small woods around Salzburg which look as well-groomed as a park in the middle of a city – I ran ahead and found a small enclosed clearing behind a rock. I put down the blanket and, proud of having found such a romantic secluded spot, I offered it to her with an exalted gesture. She sat down on the blanket, opened her skirt (it came apart on the side) and lay back. She wasn't comfortable, so she twisted her body around with a grunt. I sat down beside her and tried to see through her buttoned-up blouse and tight brassiere, then watched her bare belly and the shadow on her panties where her hair showed through the thin white silk. I put my hand on her cold, firm thigh, feeling it in wonderment. Breathing deeply, smelling the pine forest and the wet earth, I fancied that however unimpressionable she was, however often she might have been with a man, she must share my excitement. Overcome, I buried my head in her lap, and I must have been motionless for some time, for she told me to *hurry up*. At last there was some feeling in her voice – a feeling of get-it-over-with impatience.

'Mach' schnell!'

I was terribly offended.

Without another word, I got up and began to pull my blanket from under her. I couldn't have touched her for all the pleasures of paradise.

'Was willst du?' she asked, with perhaps a faint trace of annoyance.

I told her I had changed my mind.

'Okay,' she said.

We walked together to the edge of the forest, where I handed her the cartons of cigarettes. She turned towards the village, and I walked back to the camp, carrying my blanket.

_4_ On Young Girls

Your boyhood – remember?
Would you go back, ever?
Would you go back, ever?
I would not – I would not.
Sándor Weöres

Acid rain is killing the forests and the lakes, we live under the threat of nuclear war, and the extinction of the human race is a distinct possibility, but not everything goes from bad to worse. Young girls no longer seem to make a habit of tormenting boys.

It is years since I witnessed anything reminding me of the horrors of my youth. The incident occurred in the foyer of a theatre where I had gone to see _Hamlet_ played by a film star trying to prove that he could also act on stage. After the performance I was making my way through the crowded lobby beside a teenage couple. The boy must have been about seventeen, and his girl looked slightly younger. From the way she put her arm through his and leaned heavily against him as they moved along, I had the impression that they were 'going steady'. She was giggling in a high-pitched voice, attracting the attention of the dozen or so people next to them, which may have been her intention.

'I saw his eyes, I think he looked at me!' she breathed loudly, closing her eyes and swooning on her escort's arm. 'Isn't he absolutely fabulous? He could have _me_ any day!'

This public declaration of the fact that the boy against whom she was leaning with such unfeeling familiarity meant nothing to her, that he was an inferior substitute for her true ideal, did not fail to embarrass the young man. He turned white, then red. I could see that he was trying to get away from the people who had heard her remarks, but it's difficult to advance in a crowd with a rather plump girl on your arm. He was trapped among us. The girl had no idea of the incongruousness of her behaviour and seemed to enjoy our curious glances. Perhaps she thought we were picturing how absolutely fabulous she would look leaning against the glamorous actor.

In all likelihood, the boy had gone to considerable trouble and expense to bring his little friend to the theatre. He didn't necessarily expect gratitude, but he must have hoped that taking her to see a famous star, in the company of an elegant theatre audience, would make him more impressive in her eyes. Now, since he couldn't disappear, he attempted to laugh off the incident with a foolish grin, with a nervous twist of his shoulders, looking around at us with an expression which said, 'Isn't she silly, but isn't she cute.' But as he turned his head in my direction, I caught his eyes for a second – they were the eyes of a maimed dog. Seeing him trapped in the crowd, in the girl's arm, in his own awkwardness and humiliation, I had to suppress an impulse to draw him aside and offer him, as one man to another, my sympathy and solidarity.

My own encounters with young girls were positively ghastly. However, before I tell you about them I should give a brief account of myself from the time I left the US Army camp in Austria in the summer of 1946.

Colonel Whitmore, the camp commander, wanted to adopt me and take me home to join his children in Chicago, but I declined his kind offer. He listened sadly as I told him I was sure that my verse play would make me a million and I would soon be richer in Budapest than he was with his hotels in America. He had the seventy-five hundred dollars he'd saved for me sewn into the lining of my windbreaker, and made me promise I wouldn't brag about it to the Russian guards when I left the Western Occupation Zone.

I returned to Hungary on a Red Cross train and rejoined my mother in Budapest, where she had moved to get a better job. With the help of the American money I had brought, she rented and furnished an apartment for us in a majestic old building on the top of Rosehill in Buda. Having no friends or relations in the capital, we lived at first a rather solitary life. While my mother was at the office, I was at school, and in the evenings we used to go out for dinner and to see a play or a film. Although she handled our money, on such occasions she let me carry the purse and pay our way. I was by this time a tall boy looking older than my age, and it pleased me tremendously to be seen with such an impressive woman as my mother. At forty she was still beautiful and must have had her own life – just as I had my private dreams and pangs – but we had a kind of friendship which is perhaps only possible between a widow and her son. She absolutely forbade me to show my verse play to anyone, saying that we didn't need the money just yet. Still, she read with interest everything I wrote, and often bolstered my confidence by asking me what books she should read. But I was no longer young enough and not yet old enough for her to confide in me everything that was in her heart. Nor did I feel I could discuss with her my urgent problems concerning women.

In this respect, returning to the peaceful life of a school-boy was as great a shock as leaving it had been two years before. There were no more friendly ladies to touch casually when they came to visit my mother, there were no more prostitutes to contemplate. I had to face the teenage girls.

Of course I seized every opportunity of doing so. The most painful and bewildering occasion I recall was a school dance – the kind of affair I would have attended in Chicago if Colonel Whitmore had adopted me. In Hungary there were separate schools for boys and girls, but we too had our mixed parties in the gym. The visually rather impressive difference came from the fact that our get-togethers were sponsored not by the PTA but by the Communist Youth Organization. Our modern gym was decorated for the dance not only with crêpe paper and balloons but with huge pictures of Marx, Lenin and Stalin, who glared down at us from the top of the climbing ropes. Oddly enough, the tunes we danced to were American, often the same ones the GIs had played in the camp. They were chosen by the physical education instructor, who sat in a corner with the school's record player, resolutely ignoring our little indecencies.

On that late Friday afternoon, I paired off with a slim brunette named Bernice. I asked her to dance because of her quick dark glances, which gave me hope that something might happen between us. Otherwise, she was unattractive. She had a thin, undernourished face, and her body was all bones. I could feel her tiny breasts only when we were dancing so close together that I also felt the sharp buttons on her blouse. Stepping back and forth to the music, she giggled with excited satisfaction as I kissed her on the neck below the ears. I asked her for a date the next afternoon, and we decided to go and eat pastries at the Stefania Cukrászda. As we danced on, I drew my head back a little and pressed my lower body against hers. Bernice stopped giggling and pressed herself forward, and also began to shift from side to side. After a while the inevitable happened: I began to grow hard against her belly. First she blushed and made a grimace, then drew back a little. Later, as she couldn't help feeling me even with a slight distance between us, she pushed me away and started to giggle hysterically. She ran and left me standing alone in the middle of the gym.

I found her sitting on the leather-topped vaulting horse by the wall with a group of her friends, all of them talking and tittering. I reached them just as one of the other girls let out a cry of shock. 'Oh, no, no!' she shrieked, and put her hands over her mouth. When they noticed me they broke up in a fit of horrified giggles, as if they had all gone crazy. I asked Bernice to come back to the dance floor, but she refused. Still heated and wrought up, I turned defiantly to one of the other girls. She dismissed me with contempt: 'I wouldn't dance with *you*!'

One of the horrors of being very young is that you don't know when you're beaten. I proceeded to ask each and every girl sitting on the vaulting horse to come and dance with me, and collected a firm no from each of them. One of the girls slipped off the vaulting horse and scurried about the dance floor, spreading the news of my erection. As the record was being changed, I started out towards several girls who had just left their partners, but they burst out laughing and blushed at the sight of me. I couldn't comprehend what was so ridiculous or terrible about my wanting that stupid bony Bernice. It was perfectly normal, I insisted to myself, yet I felt like a pervert. I slunk out of the gym and went home, in a very gloomy mood.

There was another episode that I still can't recall without the taste of humiliation. Acting on the dangerous and idiotic assumption that plain girls must be, by necessity, kinder and more modest than beautiful ones, I once invited a truly ugly girl to a movie. At the appointed time, I was waiting for her in front of the theatre, neatly dressed and with a fresh haircut. She showed up fifteen minutes late and in the company of two of her friends. When they saw me they began tittering, and then just passed by me without even returning my greeting. In all truth, they couldn't have said a word even if they had wanted to. They were giggling so hard that they couldn't even walk straight – they looked as if they were going to break in the middle. Looking after them in complete bewilderment and with killing shame, I overhead my ugly girl say: 'See, I wasn't lying, I *did* have a date.'

I went into the movie by myself, and cried in the dark. Why had they laughed? Was I repulsive? What was so funny?

There were luckier times, of course, when the girls kept their dates and even permitted themselves to neck with me. It was like being on a plane that zooms back and forth along the runway and never takes off. I began to feel unattractive, unwanted and helpless. And how else could you possibly feel after a girl bathes her tongue in your mouth and then firmly withdraws it, as if one mouthful of you were more than enough? My classmates must have had equally unnerving experiences, for we all seemed to resent girls even while we were obsessed with them. And it didn't take much to turn our passion into hostility.

One morning I came late to school and found the class in a ferment. There was no sign yet of the teacher, and one of the boys stood at the blackboard, busying himself with a red chalk. In letters two feet high and one foot wide, he was covering the black surface with the most obscene word in the Hungarian language. It was a synonym for vagina. The rest of the class were sitting at their desks, trying to say the red word in unison, half-jokingly and falteringly at first. *Pi-na! Pi-na!* To give weight to the word, they began to stamp their feet on the floor and pound their fists on the desks. Their faces red with excitement and physical strain, they were soon roaring the word wildly, yet with a fine feeling for its rhythm. As they stamped their feet the dust rose from the floor, giving the final touch of a storm to this sudden eruption. *Pi-na! Pi-na!* The boys were getting their own back for all those questions like 'What do you think you're doing?' and 'What *more* do you want?' As they stamped their feet, pounded their desks and bellowed the forbidden word, there was no question what they all meant and wanted. Or rather, what *we* all meant and wanted, for I had rushed to my place and joined the gang. I could feel the floorboards loosening and the walls shaking as the whole building echoed our battle-cry: *Pi-na! Pi-na! Pi-na!* One of the rattling windows burst open and the red word flew out into the street. In this quiet part of old Buda, with low buildings and almost no daytime traffic, our voices must have carried a long way indeed, stopping old ladies, housewives, and postmen doing their rounds. This pleasant thought about the outside world listening in wonderment and anxiety inspired us to still greater efforts. As the window flew open, we all began to roar even louder. Yet the meaning was not obscured by the volume, it was not just a muffled and equivocal roar, it was the Word, unmistakably clear and real, sent forth to bring down the school, the city, and give heart attacks to our enemies and friends alike. Our classroom was on the second floor, and I expected us all to plunge through to the ground, on top of the eighth grade. But I kept on stamping my feet and pounding my fists so hard that they hurt for days afterwards.

Finally the principal rushed into the room. He came to a sudden stop when he saw us, as if paralysed with horror. He began to shout at us, but while we saw his lips moving, we couldn't hear his words. *Pi-na!* drowned out his voice. Not until two policemen appeared in the doorway did he succeed in quieting us down. After a brief and tense lull, during which the dust settled back on the floor and in our throats, he asked in a weak voice: 'Have you all gone insane?'

The two policemen remained in the doorway and listened to the principal's little speech, with nods of approval and slight headshakings of feigned shock. The principal was a thin, fair and pitifully balding man whom we had nicknamed the Queer, although we knew that he had a wife and five children and also carried on an affair with his secretary. A progressive educator, he tried to explain to us what a childish thing we had done. He didn't preach about sin and obscenity, he lectured about the social consequences of rudeness and lack of consideration for others, and the necessity of adhering to reason. Yet he himself was in such an irrational state of mind that he went to the open window and closed it, as if in a futile attempt to keep our Word inside the room, so long after it had flown away. As a matter of fact, he was so tangled up that once he failed to quote us in an appropriately roundabout way: he actually pronounced the Word himself. This evoked but a small brief tremor. We felt tired and smug, satisfied that we had made our point.

We later heard that our maths teacher, whose absence from the classroom had been brought to the principal's attention in such a dramatic manner, was deprived of a week's pay. But why should the principal punish the maths teacher? He should punish those nervously giggling horrors, I thought, those shy little angels who get shocked so easily.

My mother didn't share my opinion of girls. Whenever I confided to her my more innocent problems – like my date showing up with other girls and then just walking past me – she told me not to worry. 'These things will pass – they're all part of growing up,' she used to say. But I didn't want to wait for my problems to pass – I wanted to get rid of them.

The sensation in Budapest at the time was Claude Autant-Lara's film *Devil in the Flesh*, which I went to see at least a dozen times. It was about the love affair of a young boy and an exquisite and passionate older woman, and as I watched Micheline Presle actually coaxing Gérard Philipe to make love with her, I decided that my problem was that my dates were *too young*. We were labouring under the strain of our combined ignorance. Our English teacher told us that *Romeo and Juliet* was about the power of youthful love triumphing over death. When I read the play, I was convinced that it was about the power of youthful ignorance triumphing over love and life. For who else but two dumb kids would manage to kill themselves just at the moment when they were finally brought together, after so much trouble and intrigue?

And I still think that boys and girls should leave each other alone, if they have a choice. Today girls are more compliant – all too compliant for their own good – and it is they who get hurt more often than the boys. But in either case adolescence can be hell. So why share it?

Trying to make love with someone who is as unskilled as you are seems to me about as sensible as going into deep water with a person who doesn't know how to swim either. Even if you don't drown, you'll get a nasty shock.

Why get hurt? Whenever I see a man reaching out for a woman with painful uncertainty – as if he had something to apologize for, as if he expected her to suffer his desire instead of sharing it – I wonder whether girls used to snub him.

And why is it that so many men seem to think of women as their enemies? Hearing men laugh when something vicious or vulgar is said about women, I feel as if I were back in that classroom riot, when we tried to bring down the walls of Buda with the greatest obscenity we could think of. But that riot had nothing to do with any real faults of women – it was inspired by the fact that young girls were upset by the strange sight of a boy's flag flying.

I did know one girl who wasn't so easily upset. We were both fifteen at the time, but Julika was taller and less confused than I was. 'András, you mustn't jump to conclusions about people,' she often warned me. 'You're in too much of a hurry about everything.' A straight, level-headed brunette with braids. We met in the fall, and I remember going to visit her on a cheerful winter afternoon when the snowflakes appeared to float in the sunny air instead of falling to the ground. It must have been shortly after Christmas, for the decorated tree was still standing in their living room. Her parents weren't home, and Julika served me tea and walnut cake and showed me her presents, including a silk nightgown which she had received from her mother. After some heated necking on the couch, I persuaded her to model it for me. I waited in the living room while she withdrew to put it on, which seemed to take a very long time. At last Julika reappeared in her pink silk nightgown. She was nude for all purposes of visibility in the transparent material, but it covered her body from neck to feet, which must have comforted her. She moved about with perfect composure and kept turning around so that I could admire the folds of the skirt. I could finally see her long, long slim legs right to the top. At first her heavy brown braids hung down in front, but when she tossed them back I could also make out her nice pear-like breasts. They rounded out downwards and the nipples stuck two dark points into the silk. She had a large and rich mouth and a funny nose which she could wiggle from side to side – it was a sign that I should kiss her. We began fondling again and soon found ourselves in her parents' bedroom, on their wide bed. I pulled off her silk nightgown and dropped it on the floor. Julika was as willing as I was, but perhaps more anxious and fearful about what was going to happen. She was lying on top of the bedspread, her long cool legs invitingly apart, but otherwise motionless. She opened and closed her eyes nervously and smiled heroically, and began to shake.

'Julika, you're afraid of me,' I said, myself lost and nervous, and perhaps looking for an honourable way out. 'If you don't want me to do it, I won't. I don't want to rape you.'

'Oh, no, don't be silly. I'm just a little jittery,' she insisted. As her fingers inadvertently touched my erect penis she put her hands behind her small bottom and turned her head away, whispering almost inaudibly: 'Don't mind me, just go ahead.'

I tried to enter her, but she was so tight that I couldn't. So we began kissing again, but warily, and with long pauses in between – not at all as we had in the living room or on the dark streets at night. Every so often I tried to push my way in, but not knowing how to go about unlocking a woman, and receiving no help from her apart from her jittery willingness, I failed repeatedly. The worst of it was that after a while Julika grew absolutely calm. She looked at me with slightly wider-than-usual eyes, but was no longer fearful or shaking: she lay on the green bedspread motionless and relaxed – slightly bored, I thought. After half an hour or so, I began to sweat from my futile efforts and my shame.

'It's cold,' Julika said, sitting up. 'I'd better put my nightie back on.' When I tried to excuse myself, she cut me short with a sisterly kiss. 'I guess it was too cold for you too. We'll try it again in the spring.' We lay there for a while, stroking each other's arms, and when she finally got up to go and dress in her own room – asking me to straighten the bed in the meantime – she did a little pirouette in the doorway, 'But it is a pretty nightie, isn't it?'

I agreed gratefully, deciding that she wasn't mad at me. But how did I make her feel about herself? I was to call her the next day, but I did not, neither the next day nor ever again. I was ashamed to face her.

Which is to say that young girls should show their nighties to older men.

5 On Courage and Seeking Advice

My leader leads me from within.
Attila József

It got so I would nearly lose my mind when a woman was pressed against me on a crowded bus. I tried to concentrate on my studies, and acquired the earnest look of all those dedicated students whose minds dwell only upon Important Matters and rape. I had a friend, a pint-sized musical genius with glasses: he was fifteen, too, but he was already in his last year at the Academy of Music as a conductor. I read in the newspaper some weeks ago that he had a triumphant concert in Milan. Back in the old days we used to masturbate together, without much joy. I'll never forget him in my room one evening as he interrupted his conducting and let go of his baton with a cry of despair: 'Hell, you need a woman for this!'

And all this time I already knew the woman who was to be my first lover – had known her, in fact, ever since I came back from Austria. In our spacious baroque apartment building there lived also a middle-aged couple named Horvath, whom I met in the elevator soon after we moved in. They both approved of my interest in literature and encouraged me to borrow books from them; but since Mr Horvath was away from home a great deal of the time, I actually used to get the books from his wife, Maya. She was an economist by training, but didn't work, and was usually at home in the afternoons. She never invited me to sit down, but when I had decided what I wanted, she would hand me the books with some friendly remark. I was tremendously impressed by her casual way of referring to centuries as if they were people.

'This is a bad century,' she once told me. 'You shouldn't read these modern novelists – they're strictly inventors. Stendhal, Balzac, Tolstoy – they can tell you a lot about how people feel and think about things.'

Thanks to her I became an enthusiastic fan of the nineteenth-century French and Russian novelists, and they taught me a great deal about the women I was to meet in my life. One thing I learned from them was that women were often attracted by a young man's awkwardness and inexperience. Thus I finally brought myself to confess my ignorance to Mrs Horvath. I decided to ask her advice about girls and the ways and means of seducing them.

I ran into her one Saturday morning in the wildly decorated and high-arched entrance hall of our apartment building. The sun was beaming through the tall open doorway, lighting up the dust on the stones and in the air. She was taking some letters out of the mailbox.

'You're growing fast, András!' she said when she saw me. 'You'll soon be taller than I am!'

She asked me to stand beside her, and indeed we were the same height. It struck me that Mrs Horvath was shorter than many of the teenage girls I was going out with. That made me look at her. I didn't see much of her though, for I was experiencing one of those swooning sensations and the cramps in my stomach which always overcame me whenever I stood close to a woman, even an unattractive stranger on a bus. I do recall noticing her delicate bony wrist and the colour of her dress, which was yellow. But I can see Maya clearly now, the way she always looked: a small, dark woman in her early forties, with a most peculiarly beautiful figure. She was thin and delicately boned, but had large breasts and hips – enormous in contrast to the rest of her body, yet still in pleasing harmony with it. Her body was Western dualism in the flesh: with her soft face, light lips and thin shoulders she appeared an elusive and sublime creature (perhaps that was why it had taken me so long to wonder about her as a woman) but her affirmative breasts and buttocks manifested an earthbound voluptuousness.

As she walked back to the elevator – that old and romantic elevator of carved wood and glass, where we used to bite into each other later on – she remarked with a trace of concern: 'You're growing too fast. Watch you don't get consumption.'

I was on my way out to an early and, as I well knew, pointless date. I watched her until the elevator doors closed, and for the first time I tried to imagine her nude. I began to wonder whether she loved her husband. They had no children, they had been married for more than ten years – and did I not know from reading novels what ten years of marriage could do to people?

After supper I took back their books, which I hadn't finished reading. Although it was a Saturday evening, she was alone.

'I'm having some espresso, won't you join me?' she asked. 'I was just thinking this afternoon that it was rather rude of us, never inviting you to sit down before.'

'I'm not complaining!' I protested happily.

It was also the first time she remarked on her husband's absence. 'Béla had to go back to the office – they make him work too hard.'

She led me into their big living room, which I had always liked: two walls were covered with books up to the ceiling, there were shaded lamps, small gold armchairs, and a great many little tables. It was a room furnished in the modern manner, but had the light elegance of antiques and soft colours. As we sat down to have coffee, at opposite ends of a long, low table, in those smallest possible armchairs, she asked me how I was getting along at school. I told her that school was fine but the girl I was going out with was driving me crazy with her giggling. Not really expecting an answer, I watched her covertly as she poured the coffee: the two top buttons of her yellow velvet housecoat were undone, but the material held together above her breasts.

'Maybe she's giggling because you make her nervous,' she said. 'When I was young I used to titter a lot myself.'

'You're too intelligent for that,' I insisted. 'You couldn't possibly have giggled all the time.'

'Well, I suppose I didn't when we were kissing.'

Perhaps if I hadn't been reading *Anna Karenina* I wouldn't have been struck by the fact that she was referring to such an intimate matter as kissing to a strange kid who came to borrow books. But as it was, I felt this small confidence must have meaning. I began to hope.

'My girls giggle even when they're kissing,' I lied, wanting her to realize that I had got at least that far with women.

However, Maya was apparently more interested in the general problem. 'I suppose it's more unnerving to be a boy than a girl,' she conceded. 'It's the boys who have to make fools of themselves.'

'That's my trouble. I don't like to make a fool of myself.'

She looked at me in that detached but friendly manner of hers. Very unlike a mother, but perhaps like an intelligent and sympathetic social worker.

I took a deep breath and plunged in. 'I can't get her to make love with me.' This was to be a casual statement, but my voice got shaky midway through the short sentence.

'That often happens to grown-up men, too. So you shouldn't be too upset about it.' She seemed to be amused about something.

'But I've never had a lover, so it's worse for me,' I countered boldly. 'My problem is, I don't know women well enough. I don't know what to say at the right moment. I suppose I should ask you. You're a woman, you must know.'

'You should talk with my husband. He might be able to give you some advice.'

I decided that her husband had a mistress and that she knew it.

'Why, does he have a girl friend?'

Less amused, but with a greater interest in me (or so I

felt), she gave me a meditative smile. From this conversation, I remember most vividly her face: I was struck by how expressive it was. One of my chief irritations at the time was the blankness of the faces of my young girl friends. As soon as they got nervous, their faces became tight, smooth masks: there were no lines on them to turn this way or that way, giving me a clue as to what they were thinking. But Maya's face, with the fine lines of her forty some years, expressed all the shades of her thoughts and emotions. And while her ironic expression wasn't the one I was hoping for, still it helped me to keep my balance on the edge of the small armchair.

'Let's see,' she said thoughtfully, 'what could I tell you about girls? Something helpful.'

'Just tell me what you think – why wouldn't a girl want to go to bed with me?'

'I suppose you're too nervous.'

For a while after that I was silent, listening to my heart beating, loud as a bell.

'But I don't think you'll have much trouble. You're a handsome boy.'

This soothing remark gave me enough strength to get up. I went around to her end of the low table to pour myself some more coffee, and crouched at her feet. Her face looking down at me was now curious: it was a kind of relaxed curiosity, but with a warm glint in the eye. I felt she was waiting for me to do something. I wanted to touch her leg, but my arm didn't feel capable of reaching out. It was as if the muscles had suddenly lost contact with the nerve centre – I had the sensation that I was only wearing my limbs like my clothes, that they didn't really belong to my body. To overcome my stupid fear, I tried to remember all the bleeding and dead people I had seen on the road to Salzburg. I tried to think of Hiroshima, World War III, I tried to convince myself that compared with all the catastrophes of the world, this business was minuscule. At worst, she would say 'Leave me alone,' or something like that. It would certainly be just a minor event. But all I could do was brush her ankle, as if by accident, then straighten up quickly.

I asked for two other books and went home. There'll be a next time, I told myself. She's obviously attracted to me, otherwise she would have thrown me out.

I went to bed exhausted and depressed.

Next day I had a date with Agi, the girl with whom I was so furtively necking at the time. I took her to a movie, and told her I had fallen in love with someone else and thought we shouldn't see each other any more. I broke the news while the feature was being screened, hoping that Agi wouldn't argue and disturb our neighbours, and indeed she didn't. Later on she even laughed at the celluloid jokes. This convinced me how little she cared for me. I was ashamed of the way I kept chasing after her for what she would not give. But as soon as we came out of the movie, while we were still in the foyer, she began giggling nervously.

'I thought you were in love with *me*.'

'Yes, but you said you wanted to stay a virgin.'

'I said I'll stay a virgin until I'm seventeen.'

'That's a lie!' I protested. 'You said no such thing!'

'Didn't I?'

We stood in the foyer beside some stills of the Next Attraction. Agi put her arm around me – she had never done that before, it had always been the other way round – and began to speak in a deep sexy voice.

'Only until I'm seventeen. And my birthday's coming up *next month*.'

I noticed then, and on many occasions since, that when you're ready to break up with a girl she suddenly becomes affectionate, even if she doesn't care for you at all.

'You mean to tell me that you're going to make love with me next month?' I asked Agi belligerently.

'Oh, I didn't say that. You can't plan these things, can

you?' Red-cheeked and chubby, she was giggling happily again.

'Then what's all this about your birthday? What do you get out of it, playing stupid games like this?'

I left her right there in the foyer, and although that movie theatre was in the centre of the city, about three miles from our apartment house, I felt so exhilarated that I walked all the way home. There's nothing like leaving behind a girl who's been playing hot and cold with you, just so you will hang around with a desperate grin, attracted and miserable. There's nothing like the glorious sensation of cutting the cord of your frustrations, walking off for good, free and independent. It may seem odd, but parting from that over-weight and underdeveloped girl was one of my deepest emotional experiences. I had a physical sense of freedom: I felt strong and invincible. Possibly because I was hopeful of a beautiful, serious and intelligent woman – though she was only a daydream then, really – I felt I was cutting myself loose not only from Agi, but from all pointless and joyless fooling, which until then I had thought I could not do without. Walking home from the movie that late Sunday afternoon – it was spring again, and I was going to be sixteen – I felt the master of my destiny.

Two days later, when I took back the books I had borrowed, Mr Horvath was at home: they were sitting in the living room, reading and listening to music. I exchanged the books, thanked them and left, cursing myself. Whatever I was hoping for, it was apparently all in my mind.

Yet I went to their apartment to borrow books with increasing frequency: in fact, before long I was visiting them every second day. By this time I didn't believe in God, but I used to pray desperately for her husband's absence. My prayers were answered, apparently, and I found Maya alone every time but one during the next two weeks. I liked her better in a blouse and skirt than in her yellow housecoat: a two-piece costume gave greater emphasis to her fragile yet full figure. I thought she was the most sensuous woman in the world. She was always friendly but detached, and this manner of hers (which I've since observed in many educated women) drove me out into a stormy sea of hope and despair. She also developed a warm but ironic smile for me – she later told me she was wondering how long it would take me to approach her – which did nothing to clear away my doubts about her feelings. But the glint in her eyes was my beacon. Though it never seemed to draw nearer, it kept me drifting around the shores of her body. When I caught sight of her bare arm or looked at her skin uncovered by the open collar of a blouse (she had a golden-brown complexion, as if she had a suntan all the time), I thought to myself – now I will go to her and kiss her shoulder. I did not, alas, do anything more daring than continue to ask her advice about how I should go about seducing my date, pretending that I was still going out with that overweight juvenile. Of course everybody now seemed juvenile in comparison with Maya. I felt as though her soft musical voice were stroking me, like warm fingers, even when she said something that deeply embarrassed me.

'You don't have to pretend that you read books so quickly,' she told me one evening. 'You can drop in any time you feel like talking.'

Finally I thought up a clever line for approaching her. I decided I would let her know that I didn't care for teenage beauties any more, and then would say: 'Tell me, what should I do to get *you* to make love with me?' I planned not to look at her while saying this, and to look out the window if things got too bad. No matter how she reacted, at least I would know where I stood. I was just reading *The Red and the Black* for the second time, and I was sure that Julien Sorel himself wouldn't have been able to contrive a more disarming approach. On my way to her apartment, whenever I took the stairs instead of the elevator, I used to stop on the landing where there was a mirror built into the wall and, turning to face my image in the glass, I used to say it out loud. 'Tell me, what should I do to get *you* to make love with me?' I also practised a slightly self-mocking smile, which I thought would be appropriate. I had no doubt of my success, yet I failed to speak my line, no matter how often I rehearsed it. My confidence evaporated as soon as she opened the door and smiled at me.

After two weeks of this dreary display of cowardice and weakness, for which I despised myself, I decided to visit her right after school in the early afternoon, when Mr Horvath could not possibly be at home. Determined to speak up this time, I climbed the stairs (they lived two flights up from us) and paused after every step to postpone the moment of the showdown. I was already picturing myself on my way back down, remorseful and bitter that I hadn't had the guts to say anything. 'And this ridiculous business,' I thought, 'will go on for ever – until she gets bored to death with me. And then I won't even be able to visit her any more.' When I looked into the mirror, I saw myself trembling, and decided I was not up to going through with my line, not any more than the last time, or the time before that. I turned around and went back to our apartment.

There's a passage in *The Red and the Black* which was very much on my mind in those days. It's about young Julien Sorel's fear of approaching Madame de Rênal, who has engaged him as tutor for her children. Julien decides that he will find out how Madame de Rênal feels about him, by taking her hand as they sit beside each other in the garden – in the evening, after dark, when no one can see them. When I went back to our empty apartment that afternoon (my mother was still at the office), I took out the book and reread the passage.

The château clock had just struck a quarter to ten, and still he had not dared to act. Infuriated by his own cowardice, Julien said to himself: 'The moment the clock strikes ten, I will do what I've promised myself all day I would do this evening, or I will go up to my room and blow my brains out.'

After one last moment of suspense and anxiety, during which Julien was almost beside himself, the clock above his head struck ten. He felt each fatal stroke resounding in his chest with the force of a physical blow.

Finally, as the last stroke of ten was still reverberating, he reached out and took Madame de Rênal's hand, which was instantly withdrawn. Julien, no longer quite knowing what he was doing, seized it once again. Although he himself was trembling with emotion, he was struck by its icy coldness. He squeezed it convulsively. She made one last effort to pull it away, but in the end she left her hand in his.

After reading the words over and over again, I threw the book on the bed, slammed out of the apartment and took the elevator upstairs. 'If I don't have the guts this time,' I resolved, "I'll go down to the Danube and drown myself." I decided to postpone my suicide until it got dark, because passers-by might notice me in the daytime and fish me out. When I rang the Horvaths' doorbell, I wasn't quite sure whether I would be able to ask Maya my question, but I was certain that if I failed I would kill myself that very night.

6 On Becoming a Lover

... a springlike enchantment! And don't think I'm talking about anything else but love in its strictly bodily sense. Even so, it is the domain of a chosen few.
Alexander Kuprin

I made myself at length master of the post of honour.
John Cleland

The apartment doors in our building were about ten feet high, of thick wood covered with cracked white paint, and each had four huge concentric circles with a glass peephole at the centre. The glass and the yellow tin disc behind it glittered even in the semi-darkness of the corridor. As there was no sound from inside except the echo of the bell I had just rung, I began to stare at the shining glass and then to run my eyes around the protuberant circles, following them around and around until I became drunk with dizziness. After all this excitement and mental – I might even say spiritual – preparation, I'd come to see Maya when she wasn't home. I leaned giddily against the button of the doorbell with my palm. It gave a loud, uneven and off-key ring, which was the perfect musical expression of my state of mind; I remember I enjoyed listening to it. If Maya was out, it certainly wasn't my fault. I wouldn't have to take that walk down to the Danube after all. Thus I asserted myself, pressing the bell without interruption, with the happy boldness which overcomes us when we face danger that doesn't exist. I couldn't possibly describe the effect that the sound of slow, soft footsteps from inside had upon me – except to say that never again in my life did I press a doorbell for more than a couple of seconds.

Maya never used to look through the peephole, but now I heard the clicking sound of the little tin disc being turned aside, and I lowered my head to avoid her glance. She opened the door but didn't invite me in as usual. She stood in the doorway holding together her unbuttoned yellow housecoat, and looked at me, annoyed and sleepy.

'I'm sorry,' I mumbled, 'I didn't mean to wake you up. I thought you were out.'

She suppressed a yawn. 'Then why were you ringing?'

I couldn't think of anything to say, so I stared down at her bare feet.

'Oh, well, come on in. I guess I sleep too much anyway.'

Maya turned and I followed her inside, down the narrow hallway, which was empty except for Japanese prints on the walls. Her velvet housecoat was wrinkled, and from the back she looked sloppy and unattractive. But I didn't let my senses deceive me. I find her unattractive because I'm afraid, I thought. At the end of the hallway there were two doors: one on the left leading to the living room, one on the right leading to the bedroom. She closed the bedroom door, shutting out the sight of an unmade bed, and turned into the living room. She sat down uncomfortably in one of the small armchairs and I remained standing, keenly aware of being a nuisance. Yet my awkward situation in fact helped me to speak up: much as I was afraid to ask her to make love with me, I found it even less possible to coax a sleepy woman into a social chat. I drew a deep breath and looked into her half-closed eyes.

'I made a resolution I would throw myself into the Danube if I didn't ask you to make love with me today.'

I wondered about adding my preconceived opening line, but it seemed now superfluous. I was so relieved that I'd dared to speak up, that for the moment I couldn't have cared less whether she said yes or no.

'That's settled then. You've asked me and now you won't have to kill yourself.'

'You told me once that I shouldn't mind if I looked like a fool – you said it wasn't important.'

'It's not fair to quote me against myself.'

It was so unlike her to be coy that I heard my voice snapping back at her. 'You want me to leave? You want to go back to sleep?'

'You're too cocky . . . but that's good,' she said, with the warm glint, my beacon, lighting up in her eyes. She stood up to present me with a kiss for my cockiness. I had never been kissed like that before, and I could hardly stay on my feet. I reached under her now open housecoat to hold on to her warm body. I was ashore at last. Still kissing, she tiptoed backwards with me over to the room with the unmade double bed – then suddenly pulled away.

'I'll have to put in my diaphragm. And I must have a shower. A hot shower makes you more sensitive.'

Giving me a light, brief parting kiss on the nose, she disappeared into the bathroom. I didn't know what a diaphragm was, but the fact that she needed to make herself 'more sensitive' for the occasion hurt my pride. I can't possibly mean anything much to her, I thought, suddenly depressed. Then, listening to her shower, I began to walk up and down the bedroom, marvelling at how simple it had all been. I was rather proud of myself.

I undressed and moved under the blanket, and she came back and slipped in beside me. While she pressed my head against her firm yet pillowy breasts, kissing my closed eyes, I reached down to touch the warm well of her body. It's said that just before death a person sees his whole life in an instant. On the winding roads of the Austrian Alps between the Russian and German armies, I had found this to be true: once when I felt certain that the screaming shrapnel was about to land in my skull, I had seen in a moment, as if on a sky-wide screen, all the events of my eleven and a half years. Lying beside Maya, pressing close to her, I experienced a similar hallucination – not before death now, but before life. I saw the little neighbourhood girl with whom I played doctor and patient at the age of five. I had completely forgotten her, but now I was with her again, comparing her hardly visible furrow with my small stem. A rather meaningless difference it was, but her mother slapped us hard when she found us. I saw again my mother's fluffy friends, and felt the Countess's body stiffen as I accosted her at the shower door. I saw the mysterious shadow which appeared through the white silk of Fräulein Mozart's panties, and felt the cool and passive body of fifteen-year-old Julika, whom I could not enter. The memories of my long roundabout voyage paralysed me and I was helpless for long, scary minutes. As if she sensed what was going through me, Maya kept running her warm fingers over the back of my neck and spine until I had an erection again.

She guided me into her body and, once inside, I felt so content that I didn't dare to move for fear of spoiling everything. After a while, she kissed me on the ear and whispered: 'I think I might wiggle a little bit.'

When she moved, I discharged instantly. Maya gave me a passionate hug as if my performance had been the greatest thing she had ever experienced. Emboldened by her pleased reaction, I asked her how it was that the difference in our ages didn't disturb her.

'I'm a selfish slut,' she confessed, 'all I care about is my own satisfaction.'

Then we made love, from sunny afternoon late into the darkness. I haven't learned much since those timeless hours: Maya was teaching me everything there was to know. Yet 'teaching' is the wrong word: she was simply pleasing herself and me, and I was unaware of losing my ignorance while discovering the ways of her strange territories. She delighted in every motion – or in just touching my bones and flesh. Maya wasn't one of those women who depend on orgasm as their sole reward for a tiresome business: making love with her was a union, and not the inward masturbation of two strangers in the same bed.

'Watch me now,' she warned me before she came, 'you'll enjoy it.'

During one of our brief rests, I asked her when she had decided to give in to me. Was it at the moment when I was ready to give up and asked her whether she wanted to go back to sleep?

'No. I made up my mind when I told you that you were growing too fast and made you stand beside me by the mailbox.'

I was dumbfounded. This made all my conflicts and stratagems seem futile and ridiculous; and it also meant that we had wasted precious, long weeks. Why hadn't she given me some sign of encouragement?

'I wanted you to ask me. It's better for you to seduce a woman, especially when it's the first time. Béla's never got over the fact that he started out by paying a whore. You won't have problems like that. You can be proud of yourself.'

'How can you tell that I'm proud?'

'You certainly should be,' she said.

Thus complimenting both of us, Maya embraced me with her arms and thighs – then turned around without letting me go, so that now she was above me. 'You should have a nap,' she said, 'and let me do all the work.'

We first stopped because Maya got hungry, and while she was preparing something for us to eat, she suggested that I should get dressed and go down and tell my mother I wasn't lost. She said I could come back, because her husband had a mistress (just as I had suspected) and was spending the night at her place. I told her I found it inconceivable that he could leave her alone for another woman. 'Oh, I don't know – she's a very pretty girl,' Maya said matter-of-factly, without any sign of resentment.

At any rate, thanks to that pretty girl, we could spend the night together, and I went down to speak to my mother. I didn't even go into our apartment. At the door I told her that

I was in the building, that she shouldn't wait up for me, and that she shouldn't worry.

'You poets!' She shook her head and smiled sadly, offering the only excuse she could think of for my sinful behaviour. Bounding back up the stairs, I made a vow that the next day I would buy her some nice present.

After I got back, we had dinner and returned to bed – just to feel each other and talk. Of course I told Maya that I loved her, which I did and still do, and asked her whether she loved me.

'I do,' she said seriously. 'But you'll learn that love rarely lasts and that it's possible to love more than one person at the same time.'

'You mean you have another boy friend?' I asked her, scared.

'Well, my husband,' she answered, widening her eyes slightly. 'But you shouldn't worry about it. This idea that you can only love one person is the reason why most people live in confusion.'

She told me she wished they had children, and was thinking of getting a job as a teacher.

'When?'

'Not right now. After you leave me.'

We made love again, and then once again, before it was time for me to get up and go to school.

We could never go out together: Béla would object to that, she said, which made me suspect that he knew about us. He was very polite whenever we met and was obligingly absent most of the time. But even within those four walls we had everything we needed – food, music, books and the large bed. As vividly as our lovemaking, I recall our rubbing against each other and sniffing each other as dogs do – and especially our habit of cutting our toe-nails together, with our arms and legs so tangled up that it was a wonder we didn't cut ourselves oftener than we did.

All this must have affected my appearance, or at least my

manner: I began to notice women noticing me. Perhaps it was because I had lost my air of desperation. And while I still enjoyed looking at strange women, I didn't get cramps in my stomach any more.

At school, my teachers were struck by my new-found self-assurance, and decided that I had 'qualities of leadership'.

7 On Being Promiscuous and Lonely

Sweet is revenge – especially to women.
Lord Byron

Being Maya's lover, I was bound to suspect miraculous possibilities in all women. Her very perfection gave me the notion that other women must be equally wonderful inside their excitingly different shapes and colours. I suppose one of the reasons why older women are often wary of young men – and why husbands should be wary of virgin brides – is that even the most exceptional qualities are lost on those who have no basis for comparison. As Maya's cousin Klári used to say: 'You can't count on young people.'

Klári came to visit Maya about once a week, and the fact that I was always there apparently upset her. She wore long-sleeved, high-necked dresses to keep her slim, sexy figure to herself, and her black hair was always neat, as if she had just come from the hairdresser. She was some years younger than Maya, but her dark eyebrows cast a grave shadow over her round, babyish face.

'I hope you'll forgive me for saying so,' I once overheard Klári telling Maya while I was supposed to be asleep in the bedroom, 'but you're absolutely out of your mind to waste your time with that boy. You should be getting yourself a divorce and looking for a new husband. If you sleep once in a while with a boy like András, fine, I'd understand that – there's such a thing as curiosity. But to carry on an affair with him – that's madness. You haven't got much time to lose, you know.'

When I came back to the living room, interrupting their conversation, Klári gave me an impatient smile. I thought she looked pretty in a mean sort of way. After she left, I had one of my rare fights with Maya about her.

'Oh, be quiet,' she told me at last. 'Klári means well.'

'She hates my guts.'

'Don't be so silly. Klári is my cousin, after all, and she's just trying to protect me. She's warning me that I shouldn't count on you. But I knew that anyway – so you shouldn't worry about what she says.'

Then she kissed me on the nose, which was always an end to our arguments.

However, Maya couldn't ignore Klári's disapproval either. To justify her fondness for me, she was telling Klári what a prodigious lover I was. She made up stories that would have quelled the misgivings of a frigid nun. Another time when I eavesdropped on their conversation, I heard Maya saying that I could make love for two hours without interruption.

These wild tales must have affected Klári, for she began to look at me with that glint in her eyes, the meaning of which I could now recognize. And she began to make remarks about her own womanhood, without any relation to the subject under discussion. At one of our dinners she announced casually (but blushing at the same time) that her husband made love with her in his sleep, and in the morning refused to believe that it had happened. Whether this was true or not, I can't say. But I was fascinated by her sudden change of colour and by the way her face grew soft and disordered, as if she were making love – while in fact she sat upright at the dinner table, cutting her meat with utmost elegance. I could see by her face that her panties were wet.

In trying to make friends with Klári, I enjoyed perhaps most the fact that I could now approach a woman without feeling scared. Sometimes, as a friendly, absent-minded gesture, I would put my arm around her waist. There was nothing to it. She felt different from Maya, and just as exciting. Invariably, she would push me away with a nervous laugh. One day, while her cousin was in the bathroom, she said to me: 'You know, I think I begin to understand Maya,' but then quickly changed the subject.

There were no further lapses from decorum until one Saturday afternoon when our hostess left us alone while she went out shopping. Klári stayed because she was supposed to have dinner with us, but I couldn't help wondering why she felt 'too tired' to accompany Maya and chose to wait with me in the apartment – for what we expected would be an hour or more.

'Well, you're left in my charge,' she said with a rather self-conscious laugh, 'what should I do with you now?'

It wasn't only the laugh that made her body vibrate: I saw her face grow soft and disordered once again. There's an irresistible attraction for me in a woman's nude expression when she is fully dressed. And Klári was asking what she should do with me.

'Seduce me.'

She grew serious. 'I'm surprised at you, András.'

'Well, you asked me what you should do with me.'

'I was only making friendly conversation.'

'What could be friendlier than asking you to seduce me?'

'You obviously have no feelings and no morals, but that's no reason to judge everybody by yourself. I love my husband and I love my cousin. I'd never betray them even if I liked you. As a matter of fact, I don't understand how she can carry on with you the way she does. It's stupid and I don't mind telling you I told her so. She should find herself some nice man whom she could marry and leave that rotten husband of hers.'

'Maybe she will.'

'Well, she isn't showing any sign of it! She's already given you a whole year of her life, and what thanks does she get! It's revolting.'

I could see that she meant every word she said, nor did I disagree with her. Yet as we went on talking in this vein for a few more minutes, we were both changing colour with increasing frequency. Klári finally got up from the armchair and went to the bookcase, where she became absorbed in the titles. As she stood there I couldn't help feeling that she was waiting for me to approach her – even if she didn't want me to. Nothing but old age could have made me resist this situation. I went to her and kissed her shoulder, but she drew away.

'You're horrible. Besides, we couldn't do anything even if I wanted to. I have my period.'

It was a sincere lie. Most likely she would have been relieved if I had accepted it, but as I did not (or rather, didn't care one way or the other) she offered no more resistance. When we made love, we didn't have to move. Her body was shaking with explosions from beginning to end. Perhaps because we didn't really want to meet again (she thought I was immoral, I thought she was stupid), these few minutes had the violent sensation of a once-and-only encounter.

Maya came back early from shopping and found us in bed. When she opened the door on us, her arms full of groceries, she said with a smile: 'Oh, I guess I'd better join you – you seem to be having fun.'

'Please do,' I mumbled senselessly.

But she stepped back and closed the door. Klári got up, dressed hurriedly, and left.

After some time I ventured forth from the bedroom and found my dear lover listening to a record, reading and smoking one of her occasional cigarettes. As she was sitting in the small armchair, I bent down to her, but she cut me off before I could say anything.

'Don't look so tragic. It's my fault – I came back sooner than you expected.'

'I love you.'

'Now you look confused. You still don't believe that you can love many people at the same time, do you?'

To prove she wasn't angry with me, she kissed my nose

and then got up to unpack the groceries. She had brought home all kinds of cold meats and fresh vegetables and fruit: paprika sausage, roast beef, green onions, cucumbers, fat red tomatoes, peaches and grapes, and we ate everything, praising the food from time to time. We both seemed to have an extraordinary appetite.

From that day, our relationship changed almost imperceptibly. Maya never blamed me or seemed to care for me less – in fact, our lovemaking became more intense – but she began to have less time for me. There were more and more concerts, plays and parties which she thought she shouldn't miss. Of all people, she often went out with Klári. They had made up, though Klári was never seen in the house again while I was there.

One evening about two months later, when Maya expected me, I found a strange man in the living room having coffee with her. I was introduced as a young poet who lived in the house and borrowed books, and he was introduced to me as an old friend. Reverting to my original role, I asked for two books and left.

She showed me to the door, telling me in a whisper: 'Now don't you make faces. I love you just as much as ever.' As I kept standing in the doorway, she dismissed me with a gentle kiss on the nose. This gesture of hers, which I had always doted on, now felt like a slap.

I went downstairs and, as soon as I could get away from my mother, I went to my room and cried. I pitied and hated myself for losing her, I swore and ground my teeth. Since then, I've often been left alone to amuse myself this way, for loving women's company too much.

8 On Being Vain and Hopelessly in Love

This love is of the worst kind – it takes away your appetite.
Honoré de Balzac

Maya dismissed me in the spring. Through the summer I kept myself busy studying in order to skip the last two years of high school so that I could go to university in the fall. When I had passed my matriculation and university entrance exams I began to look for a woman, and after months of luckless passes, I fell in love desperately, hopelessly and without the slightest provocation. I was like the secretary who writes to the advice columnist about the fellow who sometimes talks to her at the office and once took her out to lunch. 'He is nice and friendly, but he sees me as a colleague, not as a woman. He hasn't asked me out again, even though we sit at opposite desks from nine to five. Dear Ann, I am very much in love, what should I do to make him interested?' Desperate passions such as these are most easily recognized by the unspoken yet obvious assumption that there *is* a way, that our idol ignores us only because we have been unable to communicate our true worth. If we could but show our real selves, the depth of our feelings – why, who could then resist us? This spirit of optimism is boundless.

I saw Ilona waving at me from the pool in the Lukács Bath, one early winter afternoon. I used to go to swim there between lectures. It's a quite extraordinary place, a renovated relic of the Ottoman Empire: a Turkish bathing palace turned into a public swimming pool. About a hundred private steam baths surround the pool, which is in a huge mosque-like chamber with a glass dome over it. The Lukács was jammed on weekends and holidays, but during working hours it was the domain of the off-beat: soccer stars, artists, actresses, members of the Olympic swimming team, some professors and university students, and high-class prostitutes. This varied collection of people had one characteristic in common, a defiantly exuberant attitude towards life. In the worst year of Stalinist terror and fanatical puritanism, the women there wore the latest Italian-style bikinis. This would have required some daring even in most parts of the West at the time; in the Budapest of 1950, it was an act of civil disobedience. Going to the Lukács on weekday afternoons was like leaving the country. We shut ourselves off from Stalin's drab Hungary, behind the ancient and ornate Turkish walls, those magnificent mementos of the perishability of Occupying Powers.

After my swim I used to sit by the pool and gaze at the almost naked women, in the moist air drifting out from the steam-baths. A lonely veteran of one glorious but lost affair, I watched their bodies parading by me, their wet skin glittering like an impenetrable armour. On that particular afternoon in January, I had been looking forlornly and impatiently at unconcerned women for hours. And there, suddenly, was Ilona, calling me from the pool. She raised her arm from the water and her friendly wave, like the stroke of a magician's wand, filled me with a violent sensation of hope. I hardly knew her and didn't even remember what she looked like, but while she was swimming towards me, a white bathing cap and two long arms, I made up my mind that I was going to make love with her.

'It's nice to see a familiar face,' she said, unsuspecting, as she pulled herself up from the pool in front of me. 'I bet you don't remember me!'

The fact that *she* remembered *me*, even though we had hardly spoken more than a dozen sentences to each other at a party, made me think that I must have made a deep impression on her. Returning the sentiment, I grabbed her with my eyes and had a sudden erection.

She pulled off her bathing cap, bent sideways from the waist to shake the water out of each ear, and flopped down on the marble floor to catch her breath. Then she turned over and lay on her back, looking up. She became fascinated by the shifting white patterns the wind was making over our heads, as it blew the snow back and forth on and off the glass dome. We talked about the varying severities of winter and exchanged university gossip. A librarian on holiday, she was the fiancée of one of my professors.

Although she was in her late twenties, Ilona looked like a teenage girl. She had a slight, firm figure with bouncy little tennis-ball breasts, clear, freckled skin and red hair which she wore in a pony-tail. Yet I had never seen a sexier woman. She had too large a mouth for her delicate oval face, a mouth with a sharp upward thrust, so that her lower lip didn't quite meet the upper one; and as the lips held slightly apart, they seemed to offer her whole body. Lying close to the edge of the pool she didn't have enough room to stretch out, and had to draw up her legs. This position gave an inward curve to her belly and that soft slope emphasized further the rise of her Venus-mount, which was unusually prominent by itself. It pressed upwards the black satin bikini pants, and a few escaping hairs, damp red tendrils, curled out from below.

'I wish I could rape you,' I confessed, interrupting my casual small talk.

'I *thought* you were looking at me too hard,' she answered, as if she had found the answer to a puzzling question. However, it wasn't a very important puzzle: her voice was unperturbed.

I can't expect her to fall into my arms right away, I reasoned to myself. After all, how does she know I won't talk about her on the campus? The talk might get back to her fiancé. I found her prudence reasonable. As yet I didn't plan on marrying her and I certainly didn't want to spoil her chances with Professor Hargitay.

'I'm flattered,' she said wryly, later on, as I was pressing home some suggestive compliment.

She's flattered, I thought, somewhat uncertainly.

Whenever I saw a woman who attracted me, the first thing I always did was to look into her eyes, searching hopefully for the inviting glint. But I failed to do so this time. When I looked at Ilona's face, I looked at her mouth, or her freckled nose, or somewhere around her eyes, but never into them. Crouching beside her at the pool for nearly an hour, I preferred to believe that the occasional movements of her limbs expressed her still suppressed or unconscious desire for me.

As she lay on the faded marble floor with her legs drawn up, she occasionally pulled her knees together and then let them fall apart again. While she hid and then exposed her thighs, the muscles were shifting under her skin as if she were making love. I watched the waves of her body, and did indeed think of raping her. The noise of the other people around the pool, the echo of their laughs and shouts in the closed chamber, reached me as an encouragement to be rough, tough and no nonsense. I thought of grabbing her and striking her right through the black satin. But since I couldn't rape her, I fell in love with her. I reached out for her slender arm lying motionless between us and began to run my fingers over it, sparingly and lightly. As I reached down to her still hand, the feel of her long, thin fingers affected me as if they were stroking me. I loosened up, relaxed (the short circuit of the body overcharged with violence) and was suddenly filled with a humbling, melancholy sensation of happiness.

'When will I see you?' I asked Ilona, as she got up to leave the Bath. Having learned on luckier occasions that it was wise to speak my mind, I had paid her compliments that left no doubt about my resolution. But so far they hadn't earned me so much as a date.

'Well, I come here sometimes. We'll probably run into each other.'

'What can we do at a swimming pool? I want to be alone with you.'

'Now you're getting really silly,' she said, covering with her bathing cap the upper halves of her tennis balls which were about to roll over the bikini top. She was flustered this time. It was getting late, she had to go, she had a date with her fiancé.

'I'd be glad to meet you afterwards,' I countered quickly.

'I don't make plans that far ahead.'

'You're not taking me seriously!' I protested.

'Look, you paid me a nice compliment with that business of wishing you could rape me. Don't spoil it. Let's just be friends, hm?'

Ilona said this with a tinge of contempt and malice, and she seemed to enjoy saying it. For the time being, I thought, I'll have to be content with seeing her around the pool.

'At least,' I insisted, 'tell me when you're coming to swim again.'

She sighed impatiently. 'If you want to see me so much, I'll invite you to our wedding.'

However, while I had learned to speak up to women, I hadn't yet learned to listen to them. I knew Professor Hargitay well, both as his student and as a fellow member of a research group, and I began to cultivate his friendship. I became a frequent visitor to his drab one-room flat, which was so strikingly unsuited to Ilona that it gave me encouragement in my darkest moments. It consisted of a small, airless alcove, a tiny and greasy kitchen, and a bed-sitting room full of furniture which looked like it had been inherited from an ancient aunt of modest means. There were too many cumbersome chairs and tables, all with shaky legs, and many small lamps with oversize, tasselled shades. The only objects characteristic of the scholarly occupant were the books and loose pages of books which spread over the place from his desk by the window. The fiancé of the redhead with the freckled skin and the invitingly opening and closing limbs didn't even own a bed. He had an old sofa which he must have pulled out for the night. I couldn't imagine the lively goddess of my dreams in this dusty and dishevelled hole.

Ilona was trying to clean up the place when at last I succeeded in finding her there. I joined Professor Hargitay on the sofa, and we both sat and watched her (old European custom) as she struggled to impose some order on the room. In the dim light filtering through the dusty window, she looked like a mysterious sexy angel wrestling with the forces of darkness. Under her white blouse she didn't wear a bra, and her small breasts rolled about most maddeningly as she bent down and rose again to put things in their places.

'She has a nice figure,' I complimented my host, to remind Ilona how I felt about her.

'She's attractive,' the professor nodded, showing less enthusiasm than I had. A handsome blond man with blue eyes, he was in his early thirties. Slightly overweight, he had the kind of fleshiness which only made him look more solid and impressive.

'What were you saying about me?' she asked us when she finally sat down, panting, on a chair. In retrospect, it strikes me that our relationship consisted mostly of my watching her while she was catching her breath.

We got into a discussion about her figure, a subject on which Ilona herself was rather voluble. 'I don't know what flat-chested women complain about,' I remember her saying. 'Small breasts are just as effective as big ones as long as you don't wear a bra. Take my pair, for instance – they're so small you'd think they were going to disappear. But I don't find this a disadvantage – men just look at me all the harder to catch sight of them.' She probably made these remarks at various points in the conversation, not in one breath as I've quoted her. Whichever way it was, she ended up by pointing at me. 'Look at András – a living proof of what I mean. He's straining his eyes so hard, he's burning holes in my blouse. The sly boy with the hungry eyes.'

'Please, Ilona,' sighed her fiancé, 'don't embarrass András.'

From the day I met Ilona at the Lukács Bath, I stopped trying to get at other women and thought of her continually and with increasing intensity. Whenever I forgot about her for a short time, her image came back to me with the sudden violence of an oncoming heart attack. I became an irregular third in their company, sometimes joining them to see a play or for dinner at his flat; but it was always Professor Hargitay who invited me. Ilona seemed to tolerate me with condescension bordering on hostility.

'I think your student friend is shamelessly in love with me,' she complained one evening, while placing wienerschnitzel on our plates. 'He's raping me with his eyes – most revolting. I think you should show some jealousy and throw him out.'

'She's only joking,' the host reassured me, turning his friendly blue eyes towards me. 'Don't take her seriously.'

After that I stayed away from them for a month or so. But was I discouraged? On the contrary: the fact that Ilona's fiancé showed more consideration for my feelings than she did inspired me to believe that if she didn't leave him for me, he might drop her for some other girl. I felt justified in abandoning myself to joyous contemplation of the days when we would be man and wife. Such domestic daydreams helped me for a while to stay away from her in the flesh. I preferred not to see her during this humiliating in-between period of her engagement to Professor Hargitay.

When I couldn't hold out any longer, I showed up at his flat at the next-to-worst possible moment. The sofa was drawn out, the sheets were damp and crumpled, one of the pillows lay on top of the bookcase and the other on the carpet. It was Ilona who answered the door. She was already dressed, but had no makeup on and, like all women after making love, she looked flushed and misty. I'd never seen her so excruciatingly desirable. Professor Hargitay was sitting by his desk: his feet were bare but he had his trousers and shirt on and was sipping a glass of milk.

'At last, at last,' Ilona exclaimed, 'where have you been all this time? Laci missed you. He needs someone to remind him how adorable I am. Or don't you think of me any more?'

Under the circumstances – with that faint, peculiar smell still lingering around the room – I found her remarks vulgar. 'I shall love you hopelessly for ever,' I stammered boldly, trying to indicate with a gesture that I was only kidding.

'Why hopelessly?' she taunted me, with a twist of her tantalizing bottom. 'If Laci would just leave us alone, we could hop into bed right away. Or don't you want to?'

I forced myself to turn towards her placid possessor sipping his milk. 'When is the wedding going to be?' I asked. I was anxious to appear harmless.

I spent most of my evenings at home, concentrating on Ilona with all my will power, and I began to believe that there was something to extrasensory perception, that she must know when I was thinking of her. I was sure that my faithfulness to her, in spite of my hopeless situation, would change her feelings towards me. But my only reward was my mother's satisfaction.

'You're much more serious than you used to be,' she decided, finding me at home nearly every evening. 'You're really growing up.'

'Mother, I'm in love and it's hopeless.'

'Good,' she said. 'That's exactly what you need. I was beginning to be afraid that you'd wear yourself out in your teens.'

In point of fact, I was losing weight. The only thing that

kept me going was my faith that Ilona and her professor couldn't possibly love each other for ever.

Nor did I change my mind when they finally got married. I was invited to the wedding, just as Ilona had promised me at the Bath. It was an uninspiring civil ceremony performed in the boardroom of the district city hall, with the Red Star and the indefatigable Stalin looming over the head of the magistrate who married them. This official also doubled as a marriage counsellor, a fact which they found hilarious and which I welcomed as a good omen. The depressing surroundings and the foreknowledge that this official, after performing the ceremony, would walk over to another room to worry about divorces convinced me that the wedding actually brought Ilona closer to me. From here on, I reasoned to myself (while attempting to beam now at the groom, now at the bride), from here on she will have to live in that awful flat, instead of just dropping in for the pleasure of throwing pillows on the floor. From here on, I thought, it will be the dull prose of marriage, that predictable serial of money worries and dirty underwear, not the brief, varied and witty poems of a love affair. She'll become bored and disillusioned, and then I'll have my chance.

I indulged in this sort of reasoning rather frequently, leading myself down the garden path without a guide and with a perfect sense of misdirection. Dreamy and self-absorbed, I became vicious, and even spied on my kind friend in the hope of seeing him with another woman, so that I could tell his wife. I often used to run into Ilona 'accidentally' on the street, but I never succeeded in distracting her from her destination.

Late one evening I found her alone in the flat. The sofa was already drawn out for the night: there were fresh sheets on it and a new orange blanket, very bright. Ilona had her hair combed out and was about to go to bed, but she told me to sit down and read something while she had her shower and got into her pyjamas. As I paced the floor, listening to the sound of the shower, it came back to me that this was exactly how I had waited for Maya before we first made love. I began to hum Don Giovanni's Champagne Aria.

Ilona came out of the bathroom with a robe over her pyjamas. 'Listen,' she said flatly, 'I realize that this is a rather suggestive situation for a depraved juvenile delinquent like yourself. But if you make just *one* remark, about wanting to rape me or anything like that, I'm going to break one of these old chairs over your head – and I mean it.'

Accordingly, I decided to wait for a more suitable occasion when she would be in a better mood. Not wanting to leave right away, I made polite conversation and kept my eyes on the carpet. I never saw Ilona in her black bikini again, yet I sustained myself in my passion for the greater part of two years.

9 On Don Juan's Secret

Genius never desires what does not exist.
Søren Kierkegaard

Is there life before death?
Anon. Hungarian

I don't want to create the impression that my one-sided romance was an altogether useless exercise in self-deception. This was the time of capricious terrorism in Hungary, when not only high government and Party officials but also writers, scholars, students, theatre directors, even ballet dancers and film extras were in great demand by the Security Police. As a university student who had published a few poems, I knew a great many people who were taken during the night. Indeed, the temptations to rave with fright were formidable, and I doubt that I could have remained relatively calm through all this if it hadn't been for my obsession with Ilona.

As you may recall, I lived in the same apartment house as my first lover, Maya. After a year or so of awkward hello's whenever we chanced to meet in the carved-wood and glass elevator, I began to pay occasional visits to the Horvaths again. Béla had evidently broken off with his young mistress and now spent his evenings at home with his wife. They lived together like two old friends bound by their common exhaustion with extramarital affairs. Maya was as beautiful as ever, but somehow less vibrant, and she no longer had her warm, ironic smile. On the other hand, Béla, a sturdy little man with broad gestures, seemed full of energy. He dropped his measured politeness towards me and, ignoring the particular background of our relationship, we ended up rather liking each other. A born actor, though not by profession, he enjoyed telling stories and impersonating people. He had been with the social democrat underground during the war, and we talked mostly about politics and the recent wave of arrests.

One evening as we sat in their book-lined living room, which held such different memories for me, Béla described his meeting with a former underground contact, Deputy Minister György Maros, shortly before the latter's disappearance. Maros appealed to Béla to stay with him in his office, for old times' sake, while he phoned the head of the Security Police to protest about the fact that he was being followed. The Chief of Security insisted that his dear friend Maros, one of his most trusted comrades, must be hallucinating, but that if he was in truth being followed it must be the result of some stupid mistake. He said that he would check on the matter right away and call back. Maros hardly had time to relay this other end of the conversation to Béla when the phone rang. It was a brief conversation this time, and the unlucky man didn't even bother to replace the receiver.

'What did he say?' asked Béla.

'He just said, "You were right – you *are* being tailed."'

As Béla described the scene, he demonstrated how Maros got up from behind his desk, how he strode up and down the room, shaking his fists. 'Why, Béla? Why?' he demanded to know. This man had helped to liquidate his party in 1948 when the socialist parties disappeared all over Eastern Europe, and I couldn't help laughing at the poetic justice of his downfall, and at Béla's perfect rendering of his bitter bewilderment.

'Why?!' Béla repeated the futile question, and ended up laughing along with me.

Maya remained serious. 'I can't see what you two think is so amusing,' she said darkly. But we found the Deputy Minister's demand for an explanation more and more hilarious. 'Why?! Why?!' Béla kept repeating as he paced the floor and raised his arms to heaven, mocking the wronged man with obvious relish. 'Why?!'

This was the last time I saw Béla. Several days later he himself was arrested. Maya got a job teaching in a high school. Whenever I went to see her, she was fretting about the weather, or the lack of good movies, or the difficulty of getting eggs and meat. Once when I asked her what I could do to help, I saw her eyes light up once again.

'Come and kiss me,' she said.

She was wearing her old yellow housecoat and, while I went towards her, she unfastened the top buttons, letting me know that she remembered how I used to start making love with her by kissing her sweet breasts. She kissed me violently as if she was searching for our past with her tongue. However, she soon drew back.

'I'm frigid when I'm miserable,' she conceded with quiet despair.

A few weeks after her husband's arrest, Maya left the apartment house and moved in with one of her female colleagues at the school.

As for myself, I was a regular at student gatherings where we used to argue about the future of Hungary after the demise of communism. I heard that the Security Police had marked me as *an unreliable element* and were asking questions about me from our janitor and from fellow students at the university. After a brief spell of horror, when I used to turn to stone at every unexpected noise, I convinced myself that I couldn't be worse off if they beat me to pieces than I was just thinking about it. I continued to see Ilona whenever I could, and feared nothing so much as her bad moods.

Professor Hargitay was less distracted by his wife's charms. He began to get jumpy and no longer looked people in the eye. 'You're fond of Ilona, aren't you?' he asked me once when she was out in the kitchen. 'I don't mean to embarrass you,' he added hastily, 'I just want to know. I wouldn't blame you for being attracted to her – after all, she's attractive. But I beg you, András, I beg you to tell me, please, if you come here because you're set up to spy on me.'

'Really, Laci,' protested Ilona, who came back to us in time to hear his final plea, 'don't be idiotic.'

Laci ignored her. 'I beg you, András,' he entreated me in all seriousness, even sweating slightly, 'tell me what they want to know about me.'

Ilona tried to pass it off as a joke. 'Leave my boy friend alone!'

'They want me to find out,' I told him, 'why you never had a girl friend who's a Party member.'

'That's ridiculous! They keep files on things like *that*? It's sick.'

'Well, you asked me what they want to know.'

'But their file isn't complete!' he protested. 'As a matter of fact, I *did* have a girl friend who was a Party member. We went out together for nearly a year!'

'Exactly. They want me to find out why you left her.'

He believed me, and it took Ilona some time to bring him back to anything like his old placid self again. 'I'm sorry,' he said at last, apologizing by way of a thoughtful observation. 'The worst thing about this whole rotten colonial police state isn't what they do to you but what they *might* do to you if only they happen to think of it! That's what unnerves me.'

Ilona's apology for his mistrust gave me much greater satisfaction. She wanted to place a kiss on my forehead, but I was quick and she found herself kissing me on the mouth. There's a peculiar ecstasy in the brief touch of dry, unprepared lips.

'You're a clever agent provocateur, all right,' Ilona commented, relapsing into her usual derisive manner.

It's said that there's a way to every woman and, as I thought I had good looks and charm, I assumed that my lack of success with Ilona was due to some failure of my character or understanding. I still had the habit of consulting books on my problems, and I tried to fathom the mystery of irresistibility by studying the literature on Don Juan. It didn't help. Molière's Don Juan had pride and daring, but was a rather boorish troublemaker; and Shaw's version suggested that to be successful with women one must dislike them and flee from them. The only artist who really understood Don Juan, I felt, was Mozart. In the libretto, Mozart's Don wasn't so different from Molière's, but the music spoke of a great man. The trouble was, I couldn't translate music into psychological insights – beyond Don Giovanni's love of life and the wide range of his sensibilities. The psychoanalytic essays on Don Juan were no use at all. They presented him as a repressed homosexual, or an egomaniac with an inferiority complex, or a psychopath who had no feeling for others – in short, as an emotional cripple who would find it difficult to seduce a girl on a desert island. I didn't see how I could get closer to Ilona by emulating his example.

I owe my recovery from hopeless love, and discovery of the secret, to a woman who took me for a Don Juan.

Zsuzsa was a rather dumpy housewife of forty. I used to see her at parties, where she would unnerve other guests by greeting them with cries of relief. 'I'm so glad to see you! I heard rumours that you'd been arrested!' She also reminded us of the possibility of the Chinese taking over Hungary, and warned us of our imminent obliteration by American nuclear bombs. 'I ask you,' she said loudly once as the party was warming up and her husband was patting the bottom of another woman, 'I ask you – what has the fight against communism got to do with the incineration of this country? Why are the Americans going to bomb *us*? Haven't we suffered enough from the Russians?' Her husband was an outstanding construction engineer, a handsome, tall fellow with an easy manner and varied interests – a great conversationalist and a favourite with both men and women. At his side, his plain and disregarded wife could hardly have been anything else but anxious. My friends said that Zsuzsa was a neurotic, but I thought that her constant fretting about general calamities was in fact an artful display of self-control. If she couldn't suppress her very natural discomfiture, at least she channelled her personal desperation into discussable conversational topics. However, she was bound to come to the point where she herself didn't know what she was really upset about.

At one after-dinner party which Zsuzsa attended without her husband, she tried to alert people to the upsurge of hooliganism in Budapest. The usually cheerful Party press, which confined unsettling reports to the foreign news section, had recently reported the story of a bus driver who was attacked on his way home from work late at night and robbed of all his belongings, even his underpants. As this was the only domestic atrocity officially acknowledged by the newspapers, and as it took place on one of the first frosty nights of October, the stripped bus driver's plight caught the public imagination. Within days, if all the rumours were to be believed, there were few fully dressed men or unraped women left in the capital. Yet Zsuzsa tried in vain to create more than a passing concern about the hoodlums who were lurking on the dark streets. She finally decided to leave the party before anyone else was going, about eleven o'clock, and she wanted someone to see her home.

She drifted among the guests, addressing everyone but no one in particular. 'I should be leaving – but I just don't *dare* to go out by myself.' She was a small, colourless woman, who must have liked sweets: her body was flabby and loose and she had no waistline. By contrast, she had a thin, anxious face which reminded me of nothing so much as a poor mouse. Someone advised her to call a taxi, but she ignored the suggestion. 'Is anybody going my way?' she kept asking, all the while casting thoughtful glances in my direction.

I was the only unattached man present, sitting by myself in a corner, and waiting hopefully for Ilona to show up.

'You look as though you're feeling sorry for yourself,' Zsuzsa said, drifting towards my chair.

'I am,' I replied gravely.

She sat down on the edge of a neighbouring sofa. 'That's wonderful,' she added, with a timid yet condescending smile. 'It's wonderful that you can still feel sorry for yourself. It means that you're still at the stage where you think you deserve to be happy.'

'Everybody deserves to be happy,' I stated with tight-lipped finality, trying to put her down.

'Oh, I don't know.' She drew out her words. 'I don't think I do.'

'Why?'

'Oh, I'm not much to look at.'

'Nonsense. You're very pretty.'

'It's kind of you to say so, András. But if I were really pretty,' she added with a tempting smile, 'I don't think I'd have so much trouble finding someone to see me home.'

I couldn't make up my mind whether Zsuzsa was afraid of hooligans or was trying to flirt with me. I decided that I would have a chance with her. Yet the thought of being unfaithful to Ilona – and with such an unattractive woman – was just too humiliating to contemplate for long.

As I remained silent, Zsuzsa added glumly, 'My husband's working at home. I didn't want to disturb him, but I guess I'd better phone him and ask him to pick me up.'

There was nothing to do but oblige and get rid of her.

I regretted my gallantry as soon as we stepped out into the freezing November wind. 'I wouldn't let you walk me home in this weather,' Zsuzsa said, 'but I'm terrified with all these stories going around. I don't want to be assaulted by some criminal.' We were walking through the best-lighted streets in the whole city and, apart from a solitary policeman, we didn't see a single soul. 'It's not quite four blocks,' she remarked defensively, as I turned up the collar of my overcoat and tried to let as little cold air into my mouth as possible. Yet my sullenness seemed only to stimulate her. She became coy.

'I guess a boy like you must have lots of girl friends.'

'It depends,' I answered, with the arrogant casualness of a man who hadn't touched a woman for nearly two years. I disliked her for trying to flatter me when I was so unresponsive.

She asked me questions about myself, which I answered curtly but in a bantering tone. It struck me that I was treating her in exactly the same way Ilona treated me. Though I was trying to take the edge off my manner with teasing, just as Ilona did, my dislike of Zsuzsa was genuine. Even when I had taken Ilona's rudeness to heart, I had always found consolation in the absolute certainty that *she couldn't quite mean what she said.* Now it suddenly hit me that indeed she *could*, that she must feel towards me as I felt towards Zsuzsa, walking beside her in the icy wind and finding her a nuisance. I began to listen to her with a despairing sense of kinship.

Zsuzsa evidently perceived my increased interest in what she was saying: her voice lost its dull monotone and acquired a melody of cautious delight. She was talking about her children: she had a four-year-old daughter and an eight-year-old son, and the boy's schoolwork was quite a problem. 'And I can't help him as much as his father could, especially with arithmetic,' Zsuzsa said, stopping by a street lamp, suddenly out of breath. 'He has so little time for his children – he's always travelling. He's away this week again, fixing some caved-in dam.' At first I thought I hadn't heard her properly (the wind was muffling her voice) but then she added casually: 'Yes, I spend quite a few evenings by myself.'

Standing under the street lamp, and against the background of the deserted avenue and the broad and stately apartment buildings, Zsuzsa looked slimmer in her overcoat than she had without it at the party. I put my arm around her shoulder.

'Just as I thought,' she said, with a trace of spite. 'I told myself, as soon as he finds out my husband isn't home, he's going to change his manners.'

I let my arm drop. 'As a matter of fact, I'm in love with a woman and I can't even get a date with her. She's in love with her husband.'

'I don't believe you,' Zsuzsa retorted with a nervous laugh. It obviously bothered her that I had withdrawn my arm. 'You're making that up,' she went on resentfully. 'I never heard of a wife who was unfaithful to her husband if they were in love with each other. You're too much of a Don Juan to waste your time on a woman like that. I know your type – you only go after women you know you can get.'

'Maybe I'm not as calculating as all that.'

'You don't even *see* a woman until you think you have a chance.'

'I told you at the party that you were very pretty, didn't I?'

We went on haggling this way over the amount of consideration we would charge for swallowing our pride. I gave in first.

'Are you mad at me?' I asked wistfully, stepping closer to Zsuzsa. She put my head between her gloved hands and stood on tiptoe to kiss me. Then she withdrew her hands, and putting them behind her back, took off her gloves while still pressing herself against me. I could feel her heart beating even through our overcoats. In the light of the street lamp, she suddenly looked pretty: her feverishness rounded out her thin face. After getting rid of the gloves, she unbuttoned my coat and trousers and reached for my penis. As she touched me, she began to shiver. I felt humbled, attracting her so much.

'It's ridiculous what men can do to me!' she sighed, as if in pain, disapproving of her own behaviour.

Some time later she stepped back, frowning. 'You shouldn't be kissing me here. Anybody who comes by is likely to know me.' It turned out that we were standing next to the house she lived in, right under the street lamp, and I couldn't help admiring her obliviousness. Yet even after this forthright declaration of her intentions, she gave me a conventionally casual invitation: 'It's so cold – why don't you come in the house and have a drink?'

As we entered their apartment, she led me to the kitchen, where she began to take various bottles out of a cupboard. 'I don't drink,' I confessed. 'When I was a kid I got very drunk once and ever since I can't touch the stuff.'

'You're making that up too. You're not the type to be a teetotaler.'

In their shiny white kitchen, I felt confused, like a patient in a hospital who needs the doctor to tell him what to do. I wished I could just leave. Wasn't I in love with Ilona? Hadn't I found Zsuzsa unattractive only half an hour ago? She may have known my type but I didn't, so I decided to let her know best. I took the glass of brandy she offered me, gulped it down and began coughing violently.

'Be quiet!' Zsuzsa hissed, turning off the light. 'You'll wake up the children!'

As I stopped coughing, she put her head on my shoulder. 'I'm not as uninhibited as you are. I need a drink.' She ran her fingertips over my face as if she wanted to see me with her hands. 'It's lucky we met each other tonight. Gyuri's been away for two weeks – I so much looked forward to something happening! But nothing did. And he's coming back tomorrow.'

She was telling me in so many words (and her caresses only made it worse) that all she wanted was some man before her husband came home. I guess she *knew* I wouldn't mind.

As I remained unresponsive, she suddenly went limp. 'My husband says I'm not attractive. Do you think he's right?'

'Nonsense.' I began to kiss and undress her. 'Nonsense.'

She led me into a small room right beside the kitchen. 'There's only a single bed here, but it's farthest from the children's room. We won't have to worry about them hearing us.'

Standing in the narrow space between the wall and the bed, we were pressed against each other as we took off our clothes. 'I've been married for eighteen years,' she whispered, 'but you're only my fourth lover.'

'You're still one ahead of me.' I reached to bury myself in her large body.

'You don't have to lie to please me. I know how many women you must have had! But I'm not jealous.'

We lay down on the narrow bed, my back against the ice-cold wall. But as I moved above her, her soft warm flesh surrounded me like a cosy blanket and I began kissing her breasts.

'I knew,' she exclaimed with delighted surprise, 'I *knew* you were a nibbler!' Then, for no reason I could think of, she tried to push me away from her and began to fret.

'I don't think I should let you. You don't *really* want me.'

'You seem to know everything about me,' I snapped at her, 'so you should know how I feel.'

Zsuzsa's mood changed again, and just as quickly. 'I guess,' she said, opening her thighs confidently, 'you want what you can get.'

10 On Taking it Easy

Freedom is the recognition of necessity.
Friedrich Engels

My affair with Zsuzsa didn't last through the winter. Her husband didn't care for her as a woman, but he was jealous, and we had few opportunities to meet. Although she could have come to my place in the early afternoon, while my mother was at work and her children were out, we had to meet at her house so that she could answer the phone if he called. She always settled us in the former maid's room beside the kitchen. I was glad I hadn't been able to see it in the dark the first night we were together. With its high but closely pressing whitewashed walls, bare wooden floor and one small square window near the ceiling, this cell was an architectural reminder of the servant's lot in pre-war Hungary. Nor was it improved as a guest room. There were no curtains or carpets, and the only decoration was a vulgar landscape in oils, the type of green mess which pedlars used to sell from door to door. There wasn't even enough space for a chair: the entire furnishings consisted of a chest of drawers and the narrow bed. Since no one else was in the apartment at the time of our meetings, I wondered why we had to make love in this uninspiring place.

'You certainly don't want your guests to stay long,' I once remarked to Zsuzsa.

'Here it's simpler for me to tidy things up after you,' she answered.

At least, I thought, she could have said 'after us'.

For a while, none of this affected us in our moments of bliss. Zsuzsa may have had fat on her body, but that fat was burning. I could assure her with sincere enthusiasm that she had no reason to feel inferior to any other woman. However, I wasn't speaking the whole truth. Her popular husband seemed to have done a thorough job of destroying her self-confidence, and a brief rendezvous with a nineteen-year-old boy could do little to restore it. Zsuzsa's grace and fire were gifts of an unusual moment. Under normal circumstances she looked always pale and apprehensive, as if she had just missed a train. She would enjoy herself passionately until she had her orgasm – and immediately afterwards would turn into an unhappy old maid. 'If I hadn't hurried you'd have left me behind,' she often complained, while still trembling. Either because she needed to slight others in order to feel sure of herself, or because she was anxious about losing me, she always managed a hostile parting remark. 'Be sure you don't brag about me to your friends!' or 'You look so messy – why don't you get yourself a haircut?' It began to irritate me.

'I don't want to feel responsible for the emotional balance of a boy,' she told me the last time we were together in that bare cell. She was looking her best, as she had just put back on a dark blue velvet dress which shimmered against her pale skin and gave her a striking appearance against the white walls. 'I don't want you to grow too dependent on me,' she went on, and not for the first time. 'You ought to get another girl friend besides me.'

'I already have,' I declared truthfully, taking this opportunity to break the news.

I made some new friends that winter. The students of the College of Theatre and Film Arts took their Marxism-Leninism course with us at the University of Budapest, and we struck up conversations during the dull lectures. The young actors and film-makers found us altogether too solemn, but they were nice about it, and often invited us to their parties. That was how I got to know one of their teachers, Imre Vadas, a sturdy cameraman who ate raw meat. He was a ruddy-faced farm boy from the Puszta, but he spoke exquisite French and the languages of all women. Imre's life-motto was: 'There's nothing so easy as fast living.' We became good friends. When in the mood, he liked to tell me about his adventures, and one of them I found particularly fascinating.

A few months earlier, he had been sent to film a village wedding for a colour documentary. At the wedding dance he saw a pretty girl who attracted him and who returned his dark glances. After the shooting Imre danced with her, but there was nothing else he could do, for he was leaving the next morning. She was the teacher of the local one-room school, and any rash and direct proposal was out of the question. She might make a scene, and Imre wanted to leave that muddy, God-forsaken but God-fearing village in one piece. 'I was stuck!' I remember him saying incredulously. 'But I got an idea. The tables from the wedding feast were lined up around the walls, and each table had a vase with a huge bunch of roses – they were supposed to be presents for the newlyweds. Why not say it with flowers? I asked myself. It was corny, but it *could* work. Even if the girl was shocked by my proposal, that big bunch of flowers would distract her enough to keep her from protesting too loudly. So I stopped right in the middle of a dance – I wanted to confuse her – and walked over to one of the tables. Snatched the roses from the vase, and went back. I held them out to her – still dripping, and they pricked me too – and I said: "I'll give you these beautiful roses, if you'll let me spend the night with you."'

'What happened?'

'She agreed. Blushing nicely, of course. Boy, I'm telling you, those roses were worth it.'

This story made a tremendous impression on me, and I decided to follow Imre's example the next time there were any flowers within my reach. About a week later, I happened to stop by the Tulip Café late one evening. I saw there, sitting by herself, a happy blonde divorcée who, according to

86

rumour, had recently separated from her lover. Now and then I had seen Boby, for that was her peculiar nickname, by the pool of the Lukács Bath, where I had so mistakenly fallen in love with Ilona. Boby was thirty-four and glorious to behold, especially in her blue bikini; she had such striking breasts and such twisting buttocks that I often felt like tearing them off and taking them home. She was always in the company of some dashing man who used to trail several steps behind her. She moved faster than most people. Once we were introduced at a party, and occasionally she tossed me a question when we met. She was a second row violinist with the Budapest Symphony Orchestra, a sensuous but independent-minded woman who made short work of men if they didn't behave to her liking. A few days earlier she had thrown out the sculptor she'd been living with and was now – if my information wasn't outdated – at liberty. At any rate, she was by herself at the coffee house, with her violin-case on the chair beside her. She must have come in after the concert to have her last cup of coffee for the day.

I greeted Boby with a reverent bow and she allowed me to join her. She may have been a fast walker but she was not the bouncy type – she had an air of heavy dignity, especially when sitting down. I would have gone to prison to be torn apart by the Security Police if I could only go to bed with her first, yet I was not anxious. After moping around Ilona without the slightest success for nearly two years, and then seducing Zsuzsa in one single evening, I was convinced that no woman would ever want me unless she needed a man and responded to me even before I opened my mouth. I remember reflecting happily and calmly upon the fact that only a few months earlier I would have sweated my brains out trying to find a way to attract her. Now that I knew the question was settled before it was asked, all I had to do was to find out the answer.

Boby was wearing her black orchestra dress and her round blonde face looked tired: her eyes expressed no other desire than the desire to sleep. Having no information from that deep blue source, and remembering Imre's story, I looked around for flowers. Although the coffee house was named Tulip, the worn-out old place offered no flowers of any kind. There weren't even paper or plastic ornaments on the tables. I knew that at the corner there was a flower shop which was still open; but it would have been rather awkward to rush out and buy a bunch of roses and then come back with it to ask my question. Besides, the whole point was in the spontaneity. I noticed that Boby drew her eyebrows together slightly as I looked around at the other tables: I'm sure she wasn't used to young men being concerned with other sights while in her company. Turning to face her again, and glancing at the small cracked table top between us, I wondered what I could offer her. I saw nothing but our cups, still half-filled with coffee, and a battered tin ashtray with a beer advertisement stamped on it – which meant it must have been manufactured under capitalism, before 1945. A seven-year-old tin ashtray, containing a cigarette butt from some former guest. But wasn't the issue already settled? I picked up the ashtray, emptied its contents on the floor, and held it out to her.

'I will give you this beautiful antique ashtray if you will be my lover,' I told her in a clear, firm voice.

We had just been discussing why we both thought that Kodály was a greater composer than Bartók, and she didn't know what I was talking about. I had to repeat my offer.

'I will give you this genuine antique ashtray if you'll be my lover.'

This time she understood: 'I beg your pardon?' she asked.

Up to this point I'm sure our undemanding conversation had allowed Boby to keep on wondering about whatever was on her mind before I came to sit down at her table. She may have been thinking about the disorder in her apartment, the next morning's rehearsal, or what to send to the laundry. Even a beautiful and popular woman of happy disposition must have had problems on her mind – after a gone-and-done-with marriage, after a fool of a sculptor whose belongings she was said to have flung downstairs, after a long concert – while sitting alone in a coffee house, at thirty-five, at well past eleven o'clock. Even so, Boby gave no sign of being distracted.

'I must say,' she said, glancing at the ashtray I held up for her, 'that's a proposal I've never heard before.'

'Then you ought to consider it.'

The neighbouring tables were unoccupied, and it was as if the empty space around us had become a desert: I had placed her in a position of instant intimacy. Women whose feelings are safely buried or extinct can easily cope with such a situation, one way or another. But Boby was one of those women whose thoughts involve their nerves. Things 'got under her skin', and when confronted with a sudden proposition, she couldn't help but suffer an emotional change of shape. It's not the man but the thought itself that strips such women of their personalities, as they experience an X-ray image of themselves, an intensified but reduced sense of self-awareness. Hence their annoyance at a sudden pass – they are truly 'put out'. It says a great deal for Boby's character, her firm dignity under duress, that I couldn't tell what she was feeling as I pointed that battered piece of tin at her. She found my offer wanting.

'The ashtray belongs to the management,' she said.

Content with having made my point, I put the thing back on the table. She reached for her cup to finish her coffee, and so did I – with a light heart, too. It crossed my mind to pay her soft compliments (they would have come easily) and I thought she was so close that my voice could touch her skin. I could talk my way around her tall neck, into her blonde hair, which was caught up in a loose knot; my voice could touch the tips of her ears below the black stone earrings. I could stroke her with sounds – and it wasn't an entirely inappropriate idea, perhaps, considering that she was a violinist. But why should I waste time on superfluities? I was prepared to leave the place and be glad to have spent a few moments with an exciting woman and then forget her. I even turned away from Boby to observe the thinning crowd, and met the gaze of a distant waiter, a lean, bald man who was looking at me with a knowing grin.

'What do you think?' I asked Boby.

'All right,' she said. 'But you must steal that ashtray for me.'

The strength in her voice should have warned me that the easy part of our affair was over.

This way the way to die, I often thought during the night, my heart beating happily in my skull. 'Don't leave!' she said when we first came, 'I like to feel him small.' But soon she was moving her bottom again, while her face smiled at me serenely. 'I used to be terrified of sex,' she confided in a whisper. I didn't believe it. 'It's true, honestly. I was morbidly timid and shy. Life was only my Papa, my Mama and my violin.' Then she turned me sideways with her limbs, and she kept drawing far away so that I had to thrust fast not to lose her. 'Now we should rest,' she said afterwards contentedly, 'let's do it the French way.'

She was sitting up, stroking my legs with her toes and trying to feed me strawberries, when I fell into a deep sleep just after sunrise.

The alarm clock rang at nine. Boby had a rehearsal and I was already late for lectures. We left her apartment in a rush, without breakfast. 'Let's go for a swim at lunchtime,' she suggested as we were running down the stairs to go our separate ways. I slept through an introduction to Fichte's *Wissenschaftslehre*, bought a couple of stale sandwiches, which I devoured on the bus, and met Boby at the Lukács Bath at half-past one. She had arrived before me and stood by the pool in her blue bikini, her blonde hair brighter than the pale winter sun glittering through the frosted glass dome. Strangers stared at her and acquaintances greeted her with reverent hello's. I wondered whether I'd only been dreaming about her, but my sore muscles were a blissful proof.

She proposed that we race up and down the length of the pool. When I finally pulled myself up from the water, gasping for breath, she was already drying her hair with a towel. Ignoring her appreciative audience, she gave me a long kiss.

"It's thanks to you that I'm in such good form,' she declared.

'Why?'

'Haven't you ever heard of Einstein's Law? Pleasure turns into energy.'

I suggested that we lie down for a while. We stretched out on our bellies, with our arms folded and elbows touching. I don't know how I'd missed it before: there was a long number tattooed on her lower arm. She must have seen my eyes widen, for she answered before I could ask any questions.

'Didn't you know? I'm not an intellectual, so I guess it's pretty difficult to tell that I'm a Jew.'

'I can't imagine you ever living in a death camp.'

'Auschwitz – one hundred and twenty-seven days and four hours.'

As she spoke, I saw with my mind's eye the photograph of a group of Jews, men and women with shaven heads, without clothes, naked skeletons, standing in front of a barracks; the picture had often haunted me, making me feel that if I had been one of them I wouldn't have been able to go on living even if I survived. Trying to imagine what she must have gone through and seeing her stretched out beside me only eight years later, exuding health and energy, I felt ashamed of myself for being tired.

When we left the Bath, Boby went home to practise and I went back to the university. She had given me a ticket for the evening concert, and afterwards we went to have supper at the Tulip Café. I told her how I had come upon the idea of offering her the ashtray, and later that night, when I finally fell asleep, I was jolted awake by a nudge in the ribs. 'I think I should meet that cameraman friend of yours,' Boby complained loudly. 'You should introduce him to me sometime.'

I wasn't sleepy any more after that, so we sat up and talked, telling each other our life stories. At the age of twenty-six Boby was still a virgin living with her parents when, in the late summer of 1944, the SS and the Hungarian Nazis took over the provincial town where her father was a music teacher and she was first violinist with the local symphony orchestra. She remembered standing with her mother in front of a poster ordering all Jews to move into the ghetto; her mother, who was not Jewish, was laughing at the special notice informing Gentiles married to Jews that they could dissolve their marriages by a simple declaration at the town hall and this would entitle them to remain behind and enjoy all the rights of Aryans. 'I've lived with your father for twenty-seven years – how could they imagine that I would leave him even for one day?' They moved into the ghetto, but were together for only one evening. In the middle of the night they were awakened by barking dogs and shouts: the men were to leave immediately for the work camps. There was general panic but the guards assured them that they would all be reunited in a few days. They embraced her father, saw him in a lineup under the arc lights, and never saw him again. Next morning the women and children were locked into a freight car which was opened some two weeks later on the siding at Auschwitz. On the ramp stood an elegant looking man in a white suit sorting out the new arrivals by pointing with a riding crop. When he asked Boby's mother sympathetically whether she felt up to doing some hard work, she was so taken by this unexpected concern for her well-being – after being locked up for two weeks with the dead and dying in a freight car – that she answered with a grateful smile that she would prefer to do some light work such as cooking or sewing. The gentleman directed her to the group of older people, pregnant women and children who were to be gassed immediately. Or so Boby learned later; at the time they still didn't know what was happening to them. Her mother must have thought that Boby was about to join her, for she didn't look around. Boby's first job in Auschwitz was to drag frozen corpses out of the gas chambers and stack them for burning. As she remembered, we both grew scared and clung together as if in a storm.

I told her about my father's murder and we cried for him and for her parents. The world was unbearably vile, but we took shelter in each other and in the morning I asked her to marry me. She seemed to be delighted, but put me off. 'You're lucky I'm not a few years younger, I'd take you at your word. But I've no objection on principle. If we're still together a year from now, we might as well get married.'

Boby gave me coffee and apples for breakfast, and at lunch-time we met again at the Lukács Bath. I was beginning to feel dizzy. 'You look pale,' she observed with genuine concern, 'you really need a swim.'

In the evening she took me to a party where I knew hardly anybody and she introduced me as her boy friend. 'In case you're wondering,' she added whenever anyone looked surprised, 'I'm fifteen years older than András. But he makes up the difference with nerve.' In fact, I felt rather cowed. It was a stand-up party, and I was finding it difficult to stay on my feet.

One of the guests was a prominent music critic with wet eyes, a thick black goatee and a puffy little wife. At the sight of us this man jutted his chin ahead of his chest, unloaded his spouse on me and went off to follow Boby through the crowd. I tried to concentrate on the lady left in my care, but we were both keeping an eye on her despicable husband, who was talking fast to my mistress.

'Boby's quite an unusual woman, isn't she?' remarked the wife, lifting her balloon-body slightly with her voice.

'Yes, she is,' I replied, too tired to pretend. 'I'm glad you share my anxiety.'

Then we heard Boby's voice, rising above the din. She was able to speak in a normal, conversational tone which nonetheless stopped short everybody in the room.

'Have you ever been unfaithful to your wife?' she asked the intent critic.

As the guests turned towards them, there was a sudden stereophonic silence – its range measured by scattered clinkings of ice-cubes in glasses. The critic grabbed his goatee in his embarrassment – or perhaps to protect it from the radioactive glare his wife was giving him.

'Why, of course not!' He laughed despairingly. 'I've never been unfaithful to her.'

'Then don't waste my time,' Boby declared regally, turning away from him.

As we were leaving the party, Boby suggested that I should go home and sleep if I felt tired; but I wouldn't hear of it. It was Friday, and during the night she decided that we should go skiing at the weekend. I had only skied a few times in my life, with the American soldiers in Austria, and had neither clothes, nor equipment, nor inclination to spend Saturday on the windy hills of Buda. However, Boby had an extra pair of ski pants and a pullover which fitted me, and she knew that I could rent boots and skis at the Lodge. We got up to the hills before eleven, and arrived back at her place around eight in the evening.

Boby's apartment was small, spotless and full of striking colours. Black wall-to-wall broadloom covered not only the bed-sitting room but the bathroom as well, and there was a great deal of vivid blue and orange about the furniture. Nothing seemed to have edges; it was as if the solid pieces were about to dissolve into liquid colours. At least that was how I saw them that evening, in my exhausted and exalted state. Boby boiled eggs and made toast and tea, and we ate sitting on the carpet in front of the artificial fireplace, which held the radiator for the central heating. Above it, on a silver chain, hung the now polished and glittering ashtray, as if to remind me of my once casual approach to women.

'I'm still freezing,' I told Boby, in the cowardly hope that she would excuse me for the night.

'That's wonderful!' she exclaimed, as if I had just announced some exciting news.

'I don't see what's so wonderful about it.'

She didn't explain until we were in bed. 'You're ice-cold,' she whispered, 'but I'm warm inside. This is going to be the nicest.' She was right.

We spent Sunday in bed and I could doze while she was having a bath or searching for something to feed us. But I had no more chances to sleep the following week, except in classes or at concerts. I went home for the second weekend, and took a day off now and then, but I was beginning to feel perpetually drunk. Not unpleasantly, though. Besides, I took pride in keeping up with Boby, and felt richly rewarded for my efforts. She used to walk around her apartment with nothing on but her panties, while I lay on the bed, watching – fascinated by her long white toes, those ten live roots of her whole body, as they sank into and emerged from the deep blackness of the broadloom. I can still see them, through a haze, just like then. And I can still feel the touch of her wide-awake fingers on my shoulders while we talked or made love.

If I resented anything about Boby, it was that she appeared to find nothing out of the ordinary in my ability to stay awake with her every night, and go for swims and long, brisk walks during the day – besides attending most of my lectures at the university. I wished she would acknowledge that not many men could or would do what I had been doing.

'You're such a fool,' she told me one afternoon towards

the end of May, as we were walking in the park in the last hour of the sun. 'You're killing yourself for me. It's silly.'

'Nonsense,' I insisted, with nervous foreboding. I had noticed lately that she was restless in my company, and that it took her more and more time – and a perceptible act of will – to reach her orgasm with me.

'I feel guilty about you, András.' She sounded more irritated than contrite. 'I sometimes sleep in the afternoon, you know – but what about you? This whole business is getting to be too much of a good thing for you, don't you think?'

'No I don't,' I protested miserably. 'But I'm glad you worry about me.'

It was the only time I ever saw her at a loss for words. We were silent for a while and continued our walk under the trees, in and out of the small clearings of sunlight.

'How do you want me to tell you?' she finally burst out with frustration. 'Don't you think it's time for you to take it easy?'

I didn't try to argue with her. I decided, not without bitterness, that the time to exert myself for Boby was the time when and while she loved me. I think she expected me to complain, but I couldn't do that either. Indeed, what could I have complained of, after those dizzy and dreamlike months?

O purity, painful and pleading!
Barry Pain

The big issue on our campus here at Ann Arbor is still
abortion. The undergraduate paper, called perhaps somewhat grandiosely *The Michigan Daily*, carries several letters
on the subject every day. Although most letters come from
the Pro-Choice group, there is increasing support for the
Right-to-Life argument. With this thorny problem on every
girl's mind, I wasn't surprised to see a feature story under
the headline VIRGINITY: THE NEW LIFE STYLE. A
group of second-year medical students calling themselves
MALE PHYSICIANS FOR SEXUAL PROMISCUITY
(MPSP) countered with a letter announcing their intention
to 'combat the alarming resurgence of this rare disease,
virginity, previously thought to have been eradicated.' Because some medical students audit my lectures, I was
accused at the next faculty meeting of having a hand in this
tasteless sexist joke, and to clear my name and vindicate the
honour of the Department of Philosophy, I wrote a letter to
The Michigan Daily myself. 'I was shocked by the arrogance
of the MPSP and their offer to cure young women of
virginity. If they have no consideration for a young woman's
feelings and moral principles, not to mention her legitimate
worries about her future, they should give some thought to
the dreadful retribution they are about to bring upon themselves.' There were several further comments on the subject, but the great debate died down during Gay & Lesbian
Week.

Back in my own student days at the University of
Budapest, I knew a young actress named Mici, a redhead

with long legs and arms. We used to say hello to each other for two years before we got any closer. She was supposed to be talented, and was pretty in a febrile sort of way – but too obvious to inspire curiosity. I knew her only from the Marxism-Leninism classes which the students of the College of Theatre and Film Arts attended with us. Yet I felt I knew her well enough, if only by sight and sound. She was fond of shouting obscene words, she wore unusually short skirts, and a different man was waiting for her after class every second week. During this time I had affairs with a few girls of my own age, and they taught me that no girl, however intelligent and warm-hearted, can possibly know or feel half as much at twenty as she will at thirty-five. Still, I wasn't afraid of a young face any more, and if I kept away from Mici, it was because I saw nothing attractive about her.

I changed my mind on a Friday evening in November. It was a red-letter Friday for me, for I could take a girl home for the night. My mother had gone to the country to visit her parents and help out with the grape harvest, and I was left alone in our apartment for two days. By this time we were living together more like brother and older sister – good friends, but independent of each other – and I stayed out as often as I wanted to. But it would have been unthinkable to bring a girl to my room while my mother was at home. I had enjoyed few chances to actually sleep with a woman since Boby had grown tired of me, and now that I had the apartment to myself I was anxious to indulge in this opportunity for leisurely cuddling. Unfortunately the woman whom I was seeing at the time was married, and I couldn't very well ask her to abandon her husband and children for the weekend. I planned to find a companion at the National Theatre Ball, which was being held that evening to celebrate the first opening of the season. This was the most important social event of the year for Budapest's artistic community, and it used to attract the biggest crowd of pretty women I've ever seen in one place. The students from the College of

Theatre and Film Arts were also invited to mingle with the great, and I succeeded in passing for one of them by going in with a group of my friends. It was a grand ball in an historic place – in the *national* theatre of a country occupied by foreign troops. What La Scala Milan meant to Italians under the Austrian occupation the National Theatre meant to us under the Austrian, the German and now the Russian occupation. Hungarian politics were determined by the Soviet tank divisions outside the big cities, but here we were within walls which had witnessed the triumphs of our language, the great days of our thousand-year history as evoked by our dramatic poets, the immortal manifestations of our free spirits. Both during the 1848 revolution against the Austrians and the 1956 revolution against the Soviet Union the National Theatre was one of the vital flashpoints, with unscheduled, seditious performances of the Hungarian classic *Bánk Bán*, which is about a mediaeval uprising against a foreign ruler. After the 1956 revolution was suppressed and the Kádár regime installed by the Russians, the National Theatre was demolished and replaced by a subway station. But the venerable old building which was so dangerous for a colonial police state was (and for the same reason) a potent aphrodisiac for us: while those marble columns stood they glowed with spiritual pride and lust, twin passions which sprang from the same recesses of the soul.

The foyer with its columns, bronze statues and crystal chandeliers served as the ballroom for the orchestra and dancers, the cloakrooms were turned into bars and buffets, and the darkened theatre boxes served as instant boudoirs for those who wanted to withdraw from the crowd. Many people there lived the most intense, most joyful moments of their lives. It wasn't at all like our get-togethers at the university, and I was eager to join in, but I had no luck.

I was still without a partner when Madame Hilda, a superb Shakespearean queen, made her spectacular exit.

This lesbian star was a truly royal character, who held everybody in utter contempt and had the nerve to show it, whether the objects of her scorn were of no account or men with power over life and death. Her gall was so monumental that she could get away with anything. It was well known that she had once snubbed Rákosi (the Kremlin's local dictator at the time, who had his ministers murdered for much less serious offences) *and* the Soviet ambassador, when they went backstage to congratulate her after a performance. Nor did Madame Hilda bother to conceal her strong male drive. She used to make passes at girls more frequently and openly than most men. At about two in the morning, she finally selected a couple of willing disciples from the ranks of student actresses and, patting their behinds with her firm hands, herded them away. Through the foyer, under the dazzling crystal chandeliers, Madame Hilda strode in her dark green satin gown prodding her pale charges ahead of her. Seemingly oblivious to the sidelong glances of Hungary's artistic community, she fixed her eyes and hands on the awkwardly twisting bottoms of her protégées. Madame Hilda was famous for her exits, which rendered those who remained on stage invisible.

Her departure from the ball marked a change towards a less formal behaviour. Couples content with each other began to leave, followed by women without escorts: the air had become too heavy to breathe, without someone to lean against. Accompanied by the decorous strains of a Schubert waltz, the men carried the girls off to dance or to the dark theatre boxes. Their faces still wore the stony expression of public idols, but their eyes were burning with a smouldering flame, like candles at a Black Mass. Alone in this aphrodisiac atmosphere, I could feel nothing but sympathy for another loner – sympathy and surprise, for Mici was not a girl one would expect to be left without company.

Wearing a white chiffon dress which had scarcely any back or front above the waist, she strolled among the dancers, with an air of peevish boredom. When she spotted me, she stretched our her arms with that extravagant gesture of which only an actress is capable. 'András!' she exclaimed, as if she had been born with the specific purpose of abandoning herself body and soul to me and to me alone. Before I had time to say hello, Mici put her arms around me and began to move with the music. We hadn't revolved more than twice before she began to whisper in my ear: 'You're marvellous . . . I always liked you, did you know that?' When the waltz ended she leaned against me. 'Can one talk to you seriously?'

'What about?'

'About you and me.' She drew back, looking grave, suddenly deciding that it was time I gave an account of myself. 'Listen, why is it that you never tried to fuck me?'

'I didn't think I knew you well enough for that,' I said, blushing.

'That's a hell of an excuse!'

'Let's go to my place,' I proposed, in a state of stimulated uneasiness.

Had my good luck finally put me in the hands of a nymphomaniac? As soon as we got into the taxi, she began to kiss me, and at the same time, took my hand and guided it under her skirt.

'I'm so glad to be alone with you!' she whispered impatiently.

However, we were in a taxi. I assumed that Mici was blinded by her passion for me, in not seeing the driver's slyly curious looks – as if such passion could ignore a circumstance that prevented its fulfilment. Nor did I consider the significance of her reversal of a traditional gesture, as she took my hand and placed it on herself, instead of reaching for me. I was too dizzy with anticipation to reflect. My hand deep under her pants, my fingers were feeling out that moist terrain, like scouts sent ahead of the main force.

When we were finally alone in the elevator, Mici abruptly

remembered her mother and drew away. 'My mother wouldn't like it if she knew I was up so late.' (It must have been around three in the morning.) 'She believes in the old saying, "Early to bed and early to rise, makes you healthy, wealthy and wise."'

'Don't you live with your parents?'

'I'm in a dormitory. Strictly a small-town girl away from home. My parents aren't too happy about it. They don't like the idea of me becoming an actress.'

As we stepped out of the elevator and walked along the curving corridor, Mici's face turned wax-like in that peculiar yellow lighting characteristic of apartment houses. That's how my own face must look, I thought, it's too late in the night. I felt my body charged with a current of identification. She kept on talking about her girl friends back home. I was glad that she, too, needed a pause to collect herself after our heated grapplings in the taxi. On her way to a strange classmate's bed she was steadying her inner balance by recalling the companions of her childhood, as divers first twist their feet on the high board to make sure they have a firm grip on something solid before they jump.

When we got into my room, Mici looked around to size it up with a quick and practical glance, and then headed straight for the bed with a kind of professional directness that reminded me of Fräulein Mozart. She sat down on the bed and shrugged off the scanty upper part of her dress. Before I could sit down beside her, she also got rid of her bra. Naked to the navel, she straightened her back, thrusting forward her small breasts. As I watched her, feeling put off and moved at the same time, she declared with an odd smile: 'I want you to turn on all the lights. I want to see your face.'

I turned on all the lights, sat down beside her, and started to take off my clothes. However, Mici drew me to herself, twisting her bare nipples against my jacket.

'I'd rather you'd take off my panties.'

I obeyed instantly. As I did so, her skirt slid up and she

threw apart her slim, pale thighs, then closed them again. Nevertheless, she would not part from her white chiffon dress, which now formed an awkward bundle around her hips. I tried to enter her but that bundle was somehow in the way. 'That was a sexy party, wasn't it?' she whispered, catching my ready fellow and drawing it up against her belly. She felt it, petted it, pressed it down to keep it still, closing her eyes and keeping them closed. What did she see? She saw something – I could tell from the way she smiled. Was it that she needed the extra stimulus of suggestive images, and kept her eyes closed so that behind her eyelids she could watch other bodies, while feeling mine? An imaginative girl is said to be capable of engaging in mass-copulation even with one partner.

After an hour or so, I began to get impatient and Mici, sensing the increasing weight of my movements, rolled away to the other side of the bed and crossed her legs. She looked resentful.

I staggered over to my old hand-winding record player and began to crank up the machine. It seemed as good a way as any to steady myself. With a girl who was so quick to come to the point, I felt duty-bound to let her choose her own time.

'Look at me,' I heard Mici saying. 'I want to see your face.'

I looked at her and suggested that she move under the blanket – otherwise she might catch cold.

'I can't.'

'Why?'

'I'm religious.'

'What do you mean, you're religious?'

'I'm a virgin.'

I adjusted my disordered clothes, feeling shy about my stupidity.

'Look at me, I want to see your face,' Mici insisted, and I began to suspect why.

But she forestalled any possible reproach I might have made. 'Even if you don't look at me, I can tell you're angry.

But that just proves that you don't love me. If you loved me, you'd be satisfied with just playing around.'

'Well, we have played around,' I said bitterly, standing in the middle of the room, out on no man's land. 'How about playing something else for a change? Do you want to listen to records? Just sit and talk?'

'It must be four in the morning,' Mici pouted, 'it's too late for conversation.'

'Well, do you want to go home?'

'It's easy for you to talk, you're a boy.' She drew the top of her dress on again, but not her bra, and pulled down her skirt. 'I couldn't look my mother in the face again, if I ever forgot myself. Don't laugh' (I couldn't possibly) – 'you don't know my mother. She planned to be a nun, even while my father was courting her. But then he knocked her up, so that was it.' She added with a conciliatory grin, 'I guess you could say that I was a matchmaker even before I was born.'

'That sounds just as phoney as everything else you've said.'

'And what if you'd made me pregnant? Of course you didn't think of that!'

'I've never made anybody pregnant,' I protested righteously. 'But nuns don't tell you about birth control, do they?'

'I like you but I won't do it.'

'I thought you were complaining at the dance that I hadn't "fucked" you!'

'I was complaining that you hadn't *tried*.'

Saying this, Mici couldn't quite suppress a triumphant giggle. The sound threw me right back to where I had started eight years ago, with the teenage girls.

'Look, Mici, I'm going to call you a taxi.'

'I don't want to go.'

'Mici – either you leave or I call the police.'

'And what would you tell them?' Silence. 'If you knew anything about women, you'd know that I love you.'

'All right, then *I'll* leave.'

She caught me at the door and leaned against me, sad and hurt. She began to undo my tie, asking in a husky voice: 'Why don't you take off your clothes?'

Overcome by the illusion that I was making progress, I undressed myself. She led me back to the bed by my fellow and we began our skirmishes again, both of us naked except for that moving bundle around Mici's waist. I can't recall exactly what happened and in what order, though I do remember my steadily worsening headache and some of our more violent movements. Mici succeeded in luring me back again and again, winding me around her body, but always closing her thighs in time to prevent me from entering her. I thus tried to make her while she was unmaking me. Shaking with rage, I accused her of being a sadist. Did she hate everybody or only men? And why? Had her father beaten her when she was a child? Once I called her a virgin whore, which made her cry.

'I'd rather screw with you than with anyone else, but I have to save myself for my husband.' She wiped away her tears with her bra. 'Marry me tomorrow and you can have me right in the magistrate's office afterwards. It isn't that I'm timid or anything. I'd do it right in his office. And I mean it.'

'Yes, I'm sure you'd like that. We'd have all the lights turned on so you could watch the magistrate's face.'

Mici laughed at that. But she couldn't allow me to stay away from her too long: perhaps she wanted to prove that she could excite me even after I had seen through her – or possibly she just wanted to enjoy herself in her own way. If I went to sit by the desk with my back to her, she came up behind me and began to kiss the back of my neck, the tips of my ears. When I was sufficiently aroused, we would go back to the bed. She could be the flame of passion itself up to the moment of truth – and later again. To quote Abraham Cowley, she was the perfect *outside woman*.

In all her outward parts Love's always seen
But, oh, he never went within!

Instead, she offered to practise fellatio for me. I was too sceptical by then to believe her. 'That's just another of your sadistic little tricks – you'd bite it off.'

'If I was a sadist,' she countered, 'I wouldn't offer to relieve you, would I?'

'I'd rather you explained your religion to me. Once I wanted to be a priest, maybe I'll understand it.'

'Well, you want me to do it for you or don't you?'

'I wouldn't dream of inconveniencing you.'

'I actually like it. I've done it for lots of boys. I'd have done it for you right away when we came in, if you'd thought of asking. I did it the first time when I was fifteen, with a guy who said he'd kill me if I didn't give in. I had to do something to simmer him down. I didn't like it then but now I enjoy it.'

Then, or later, we made love in the French way. We both came, but it didn't help me, my headache only grew worse. Mici was completely satisfied. It was the culmination of her chaste dreams, I suppose: the mysterious immaculate conception.

Around seven in the morning I told her I was going to bed to sleep, and she could leave, stay or come to bed with me.

'I'll sleep in the chair,' she decided.

I woke up around noon with the most painful headache of my life. I felt my brain moving inside my skull. Aspirins didn't help, and I finally ended up in the Emergency Ward of a hospital, where they decided to give me a morphine injection. However, that was late in the evening of the same day. At the moment of waking I had a clouded vision of Mici sitting on top of my desk, swinging her legs back and forth.

'How do you feel?' she inquired.

'I'm so sick, I can hardly see you.'

'I feel lousy too. You should have used a little force at the right moment.' Nevertheless, she was willing to share the blame. 'Ever since I woke up, I've been thinking of all the men I've missed. And all for that stupid future husband of mine whom I don't even know yet.'

'Virtue is its own reward, Mici.'

'Don't you make fun of me!' she complained bitterly.

How could I? In the seed of my headache was the discovery that, confronted with a naked woman, I had neither will nor sense.

'Just watch me after I get married. I'll sleep with every man who asks me, I won't care even if he's a hunchback.'

This is a word-for-word translation of her statement. I'm sure I haven't recalled accurately everything she said that night, but this declaration was too striking ever to fade from my memory. Especially since I believe she subsequently made good her resolution.

She dropped out of the College of Theatre and Film Arts about a year later. To augment her scholarship she had taken on a singing job in a nightclub, and there she became acquainted with, of all people, the military attaché of a Southern European NATO power. I have no way of knowing how much truth there was in all the rumours, but it was a fact that after her marriage to this dignitary she could be seen almost nightly with various Communist and Western diplomats at the bars of the better hotels. Her friendships actually became a Cold War issue, because she was suspected by both sides of giving information to the enemy. One of my classmates, whose father was a deputy minister in the Ministry of Foreign Affairs, told us that for a while Mici was trailed on her tête-à-têtes by both Soviet and NATO Intelligence. The diplomat was recalled by his government and Mici left Hungary with him, a few months after their wedding.

As for the turns of my own life after our unforgettable night together, I never again tried to deflower a virgin. Nor did I ever consider marrying one. Whatever else I've done, I've stayed clear of pure girls. They're fearful of the consequences; I'm terrified of the preliminaries.

12 On the Deadly Sin of Sloth

I've ruined my life through moral dissipation in my corner.
Dostoevsky

I must have been about eighteen at the time, still hopelessly
in love with Ilona and hungering to embrace any woman,
when I found myself alone one day in the deserted wing of a
university library with a girl student who later became a star
tennis player, Margit S. We bandied words, kissed, fondled.
She was a flashy brunette with red lips and nipples and she
let me kiss them and suck them, but I begged her in vain to
go somewhere with me; she kept saying, 'that's enough,
that's enough', she had no time, and then she suddenly left.
Giddy from the taste and smell of her breasts, I had rarely
felt such a desperate craving for a woman. I felt seasick. She
had stirred up an ocean of longing in me, setting off a storm:
I could feel the waves of blood coursing through my brain,
then rushing downward. Sitting at my reading table, I
masturbated quickly. Of all the children I might have had,
few could have been as full of life as the one I should have
fathered at that instant: my palms filled with semen to the
brim. And while I sat at the table with my hands full,
wondering what to do with it, Margit S. came back to say that
she had changed her mind and we could go to her aunt's
place, since her aunt wasn't home.

Today I would have confessed to her what had happened
and she might have found it funny or perhaps even flatter-
ing, but at the time I was so ashamed, so afraid she might
come closer and see what I had in my hands, that I told her
rather sourly that I had got back into my book and wanted to
go on reading. Her eyes widened, she turned, hurried away,
and became my deadliest enemy. Ever since then I have

thought of masturbation as missed opportunities. For her part, Margit denounced me to the communist party secretary of the University of Budapest, telling him I had boasted to her that I invented quotations from *Das Kapital* for the Marxism-Leninism exams, on the assumption that none of the examiners could possibly have read the whole book. I denied it, of course, but was nearly expelled just the same.

I'm reminded of this fruitless incident by a pornographic magazine sent to me by one of my students with a note asking 'What do you think?' The magazine features a long article extolling the triumph of 'the masturbation revolution'. It was sent to me shortly after *The Michigan Daily* published my plea for abstinence from virgins, and possibly my student wanted to query me about alternatives. Which made me realize something I had been aware of only in a subliminal sort of way: there were a great many young men – and for that matter older men – on and around the campus who, like the hero of *Notes from Underground*, seemed to live all alone squandering themselves in some corner. Not cripples, hideously deformed unfortunates who could have had no one's attention, but handsome, pleasing men whom many women would have been happy to embrace. The porn magazine, though it doesn't quite say so, appears to be right: if there is a sexual revolution, it is of the most lonely kind.

Next time I was asked to address a proudly all-male fraternity I decided to have my say with a poem, which I called a 'sermon', to shock them into thinking.

Sermon to a Meeting of Onanists Anonymous

I

The Holy Spirit dwells
in the precious juices of our genitals
it inspires us to overcome the deadly sin of sloth
to quicken our steps and strengthen our limbs
– the juices fill us with curiosity

the courage of reaching out
the daring to leap into the unknown.
As a man's cock rises so we rise above
our indifference to strangers
we learn to tolerate to care to love
sometimes even to understand
in the expectation of pleasure:
women open and men submerge,
thighs and foreheads anointed with sweat
and whatever positions we take we acquire
the knack of living with the living.

2
For fantasy, take two women
one a bit lesbian nuzzling deep
in the well of another whose voice
rises and falls
while the tongue-tied girl's buttocks bounce
as she backs away for air to press forward again
– and you enter only as she bursts.
Or picture the most colourful orgy
made to your most singular taste:
however rich it may be
what you conceive in solitude
betrays a poor imagination
about the bliss of a hug or a kiss.

Being the giver-and-taker of your pleasure
you grow too weak in the legs
to run after company.
Waves of solitary joy
carry you to desert islands.

3
They say the strong don't depend on anybody
not even for joy
they know the quickest surest absolutely safest way
to win.

Rapists drill with their pricks;
if their lovers are imaginary
no matter that their victims are real.
I say the strong have patience
they wait they beg
they would rather brave rejection
moods arguments the labours of love
than fly off alone
– they gamble on company
entrusting even their most sensitive parts
to the care of a friend.

13 On Mothers of Little Children

'Come, come,' said Tom's father, 'at your time of life,
There is no longer excuse for thus playing the rake.
It is time you should think, boy, of taking a wife!'
'Why, so it is, Father. Whose wife shall I take?'
Thomas Moore

The chains of matrimony are so heavy that it takes two to carry them –
sometimes three.
Alexander Dumas

During the remainder of my student years I had many frustrating experiences, but few with women. I owe my good luck to the dear wives who shared with me their matrimonial joys and sorrows. Our romances were untroubled and unclouded, there was no needling, nagging or quarrelling – after all, what would be the point of extramarital affairs if they were the same as marriage? Moreover, I didn't have to pay for their love the dues of social responsibility, at a time when I still had to study, help my mother and busy myself with all the indispensable activities of any young man. They saved me from the tragic mistake of marrying too soon, although I made marriage proposals to several of them. They also saved me from the excesses of passion; as a rule, wives are too busy to wear out their lovers. I could offer them only temporary distraction from their domestic ills, but it was joy without fear of retribution. They could embrace me without bringing upon themselves the obligation of having to wash my socks. Thus we spent our free time in happy adulteries.

Yet what stays in my mind most clearly is the misery of some of those wives, especially the ones with small children. As a rule, the mother of little children is going through the worst crisis of her life. She has had two or three pregnancies in quick succession, the periods of her husband's first extramarital affairs. His cooling ardour only magnifies her anxieties about her figure and her age, as her dream-world of eternal love and girlhood falls to pieces. She is faced with the impossible task of winning back her husband at the very time when she is accosted with another series of new worries and duties in looking after her little people. While she's teaching them to walk, she herself is trying to find her balance on a slippery terrain of new reality. Will her husband stay away again tonight? Is she no longer desirable? No one needs the reassurance of a new romance as much as she does, yet the bitter irony of her predicament is that just when her husband is ignoring her, possible lovers do the same: men tend to see her only as a mother. There she is, more of a woman than ever, and she is supposed to care about nothing but the children and the household.

Once, it is true, I knew a mother who had nothing to complain about: she had an adoring and lovable husband, five handsome and good-natured boys, and she enjoyed possessing and looking after all of them, keeping a spotless and cheerful home. Yet she also had innumerable lovers, apparently having no graver problem than a miraculous excess of energy. I also knew mothers whose miseries were so overwhelming that the sedative of an affair was no use to them. Nusi was such a woman – though putting Nusi in any category is not quite fair.

I met, or rather found, her children first. I was out for a stroll on St Margit Island (a pleasant and popular park on the Danube, between Pest and Buda) and saw them wandering aimlessly among the crowd: a grave-looking boy of five or so, dragging along by the hand a smaller girl, who was crying. I tried to find out what the trouble was. The boy wouldn't talk to a stranger; I turned to the little girl, who finally told me that their mother had gone to the toilet, telling them to wait outside, but her brother had got bored and dragged her away. They had been looking for their mother for more than an hour, and so far none of the passers-by had paid any attention to them. As they stood a good chance of continuing to miss their mother if they kept moving around, I decided to anchor them at a refreshment stand by the bridge, which she would have to pass before leaving the island. It was a hot evening in mid-July, and when I offered the children an iced raspberry soda they consented to join me. The cold drink loosened the boy's tongue and he asked for a sandwich.

They both acted as if they had never seen food before. They were in fact pale and undernourished-looking, and their cheap summer clothes, though clean and tidy, showed signs of many mendings. However, they both had magnificent eyes: large, deep and sparkling.

'Are you a drunk?' the boy asked, between sandwiches.

'No, I'm not.'

'You're just a boy too, eh?'

'I guess you could say I'm a grown-up.'

'You're lying!' he countered scornfully. 'Grown-ups are drunks.'

'How do you know?'

'My dad's a drunk.'

'Is your mother a drunk too?' I asked.

'No, she's just a woman.'

'Slum kids,' remarked the kind-looking white-haired lady behind the counter, who had overheard the conversation. 'They're pretty things now but they'll turn out monsters, you'll see.'

As the children had had all the sandwiches and soft drinks they could take, I led them a few steps away from the stand. The girl, Nusi, hung on to my hand, but her brother Joska began to wander off and I had to run after him several times.

'He *always* walks away,' commented his sister. 'It's a *mania** with him.'

---

*Mania is one of the most common Hungarian words, for obvious reasons.

'This time you stay put,' I finally told him, 'or I'll tear off your ears.'

Joska shrugged his shoulders, resigned and unimpressed. 'Everybody beats me up.'

'Who beats you up?'

'Dad and everybody.'

'Does your mother beat you?'

'No, she doesn't and Grandma doesn't – but they're just women.'

I was beginning to feel sorry for both the boy and his mother. 'Well, I'm a man and I don't beat you. As a matter of fact, I've never beaten anybody. I just wanted to scare you, so you'd stay here.'

'You're lying,' he announced as before.

'No, I'm not. I've really never beaten anybody.'

'Then you were lying when you said you'd tear my ears off.'

'Yes, that's when I was lying.'

'You mean you've never beaten up anybody?'

'Never,' I insisted.

The boy thought this over for a while, sizing me up with his suspicious eyes. 'Are you a Jew?'

'No, why?'

'Dad says Jews are peculiar.'

'Maybe he doesn't know.'

Joska accepted this, too, with an air of resignation. 'Maybe he doesn't. Grandma says Dad's just shooting off his mouth.'

I also learned that their father was a mechanic, working in a factory, that they had not only a room but a kitchen too, and that Dad often spent the night next door where there was a girl who painted herself – even her hair. Dad said that she was prettier than Mother, who, as the boy repeatedly assured me, was 'just a woman'.

When Mother finally turned up, she was a surprise. She came running towards the refreshment stand, wearing a faded blue cotton tunic without a blouse, and I thought at first that she was just another thirsty girl. Though her children were fair, Nusi was a brunette, and her thick, dark hair fell loosely to her bare shoulders. Her eyes were as large and black as her children's and flickered for a brief second as she thanked me for keeping the kids company. A strong, sexy woman, I thought. Only her cheekbones showed that she wasn't eating enough either. The children's news about sandwiches and soft drinks upset her.

'You shouldn't have bought them anything even if they asked for it,' she said defensively. 'You ought to know that children can't incur debts. But I guess you expect to be paid for it all, just the same.'

Suspiciousness was obviously a family trait. I left the island with them and – as the boy was dragging his sister ahead of us – I told Nusi that I found her fascinating. She reacted with unexpected violence.

'Christ! You must be hard up if you notice a wreck like me!'

'I hate women who deprecate their looks. It's phoney.'

'There's certainly nothing fascinating about me,' she said somewhat more calmly. Then she flared up again: 'What are you, a pervert?'

'No, I just like girls with good breasts.'

'So you loaf around parks to pick up women, eh?'

'I don't go anywhere to pick up women, I'm too busy. But I'll try my luck anywhere if I see someone I'd like to know.'

She turned her eyes towards me for a second. There were people getting between us and the children: we had to hurry to catch up with them. We reached the bridge that led us to Pest, and we were walking over the river when she returned to the subject.

'So you're one of those, eh?'

'Yes,' I admitted, 'I'm one of those.'

Then again, with cold suspicion: 'What do you do for a living?'

'I'm a student, I live on scholarships.'

'That's a nice job.' Still, she wouldn't trust me enough to give me a date. 'Why should I? I'm sure you'd change your mind and not show up.' She wanted to check her face in a mirror and looked for one in her purse, without success. 'I'll tell you what,' she finally said, 'I won't give you a date but you can come home with us. I'll leave the kids with my mother and then you can take me to a movie or something.'

That was more than I'd asked for. 'Wouldn't your husband object?' So far we hadn't talked about him. I was worried that he might take me for a Jew and try to beat me up.

No such possibility worried Nusi. 'He'll be out.'

'How about your mother?'

'Oh, she always says why don't I go out and have a good time. But I don't like to go out by myself and I can't stand women friends.'

'Do you people all have a thing about women? Your son calls you "just a woman".'

'That's his father's expression.'

Nusi had a strong and thrusting jaw, I noticed as I walked beside her. We took the long streetcar ride beyond the city to a hell of factories, slums, smog and thick layers of soot. The buildings, the billboards, even the panes of the windows were black. They lived in a five-storey building, a square, prison-like structure, and we climbed a dark, dilapidated staircase, passing several open doors leading straight into dark kitchens. The door next to their third-floor apartment was closed. I hoped it was the painted girl's and that Nusi's husband was either inside there or out of the building. As we stepped into the kitchen, I saw a sight I'll never forget. It had no window, and the walls were covered with open shelves holding dishes, pots, food, clothes and sheets. The shelves apparently served as cupboards for all the small items of the household. Besides the stove and the kitchen table with five wooden stools, there was an old armchair (the living room) and in one corner a bed, where Nusi's mother slept, as I was to learn. In another corner there was a tub set against the wall (the bathroom). The communal toilet was at the end of the corridor on each floor. As I sat in the armchair I could see into the bedroom: two beds and the edge of a clothes cupboard. Everything was meticulously tidy and as clean as possible. Nusi's husband was out.

'Mother,' Nusi introduced me primly, 'this gentleman found the kids for me at St Margit's, so I invited him for a cup of tea.'

The grandmother looked much like Nusi, except older and stronger. She seemed upset. 'I'd have made dinner for one more, but I didn't know you were coming.'

'Actually, I wanted to ask Nusi out for dinner, if I may.'

'Why, of course, if she wants to,' nodded the old woman with relief.

'Well, if we're going out for dinner, I might as well put on a blouse,' Nusi said, disappearing into the bedroom. She closed the door and I heard her turn the key in the lock, which struck me as excessive modesty.

'When will Dad be home?' asked little Nusi.

'Don't worry, he'll be home to eat.'

I tried to say that I didn't want him to miss his wife (it was a Saturday evening) and maybe we should go out some other time, but the old lady interrupted. 'Don't worry, Joska'll be glad to eat the extra portion.'

I looked at the boy, but he shook his head. 'She means Dad.'

Nusi came back with a pretty white blouse under her blue jumper, and we left immediately. I was anxious to get out of that kitchen, though later I got used to it and even used to remember it with nostalgia, when I no longer went there.

Back in the city, we went into a quiet restaurant and asked for chicken paprikás and candles to light. While we waited for our order, Nusi mused over my good luck in being able to earn money by doing what I liked, studying. I asked her what she would do if she could make a living by doing what *she* liked.

'Look after a man who loved me and raise my kids.' When the candles arrived, and the waiter placed them so that they made a glowing frame for her pale face and huge dark eyes, she added fiercely, 'But I hate daydreaming, nothing ever comes of it.' When we were served, she abandoned herself to the food and the task of interrogating me. Struggling with the slippery chicken paprikás, I had to answer the question (she went straight to the heart of every issue) of how long I went out with a woman.

I couldn't manage a reply without spilling some gravy on my shirt. 'I stay with a girl as long as I can hold her and she can hold me.'

'You mean you have one woman after another, eh?'

I was easy game for this line of questioning, and Nusi grilled me thoroughly. Yet – as I learned later – she had accepted me long before we began to talk. If she was trying to figure me out, it wasn't a pusillanimous weighing of pro's and con's: she just wanted to be ready.

'I like to know what I can expect from a guy,' she said.

'And what do you think you can expect from me?'

'I don't know,' she admitted pensively. 'But whatever it is, it isn't much.'

If she finds me so unpromising, I thought, I might as well shut up. My lapse into gloomy silence apparently pleased her. 'You're hurt, eh?' she asked with sudden affection.

'Yes, I am.'

'Well, that'd prove you cared for me a little, wouldn't it? My husband doesn't,' she said with a flash of bitterness. 'He's so uninterested, I can call him the worst names and he doesn't even listen.'

Later on, Nusi asked me about the university. 'Tell me something worth knowing, like what do you study?' She worked in a department store, wrapping merchandise, but when we talked it was like talking with one of my classmates.

She could think with precision and speed, and showed a genuine appetite for both facts and ideas. It took me no time to see ourselves as Eliza Doolittle and Professor Higgins. I saw us dining in the same restaurant several years later: Nusi wearing a smart new dress, a schoolteacher perhaps, with a pleasant apartment for us to go to. Her potentialities had been criminally wasted in the past by poverty and an insensitive husband, but she had finally come into her own. A woman who didn't expect much from me, yet I transformed her life. I decided I would.

However, she drew a different conclusion from our talk. 'Well, I guess I shouldn't worry about you being younger than me,' Nusi said as we got up from the table. 'Maybe you don't know much about life and people, but at least you know more than I do about things you learn from books. It kind of evens out, I suppose. I can't stand guys who're dumber than I am.'

We left the restaurant and, as we had nowhere else to go and the hot day had turned into a warm night, we decided to go back to St Margit Island. We took the bus to the Danube and walked across the bridge, hand in hand. The river smelled fresh as a mountain brook. There was a pale moon and the soft dark mass of the island lay ahead of us like a huge bed, with the puffy black mounds of trees for pillows. Maybe Nusi had similar associations, for she suddenly stopped.

'I warn you, you won't get anywhere with me tonight. I wouldn't sleep with a guy unless I'd known him for at least a month.' She was ready to turn back and wouldn't go on until I succeeded in convincing her that I accepted her terms. 'You need a woman like me to set you straight,' she concluded.

The island was quiet and apparently deserted. There may have been other couples about but if so they had hidden themselves well. If Nusi wanted to know everything about me, she was also willing to tell everything about herself. She was bitter and desperate about what she was saying, yet her manner of saying it was almost cheerful. Her marriage began to go wrong when she first got pregnant. 'He knew I was pregnant but he kept railing at me for looking fat. It was driving me crazy, all his cracks about my figure. It was his own child and all he had to say was that I was a fat woman.' Things seemed to improve for a time after their son was born: József became considerate again. He even decided to work overtime, to stay in the factory until midnight, putting aside money for his son. Nusi felt confident until a woman friend brought the news that József was doing overtime with a girl, not at the plant. By the time their daughter was born, he didn't even try to make up stories when he stayed out. 'When he didn't even try to lie any more I knew I'd had it.'

'Why don't you divorce him?'

'For whom?' she asked, looking me over.

I couldn't resist kissing her for her practical turn of mind, and she returned the kiss with her thick, soft mouth. It was more questioning than her question. As we went on walking hand in hand, along the moonlit paths and through the cool deep grass, it was possible to imagine that we would start a new life together.

Her job didn't pay well, but József had lately been bringing home his pay cheque – ever since he'd started sleeping with the bitch next door. 'She's the one who wants us to have his money – she doesn't want to fight us in the hall, she's afraid of the neighbours talking.' József still ate his meals at home and kept his things there. 'Sometimes he still sleeps with me when he's so drunk he doesn't know what he's doing.'

When we got tired of walking we sat down under a giant oak surrounded by bushes. Nusi leaned back against the tree. We began kissing and I reached my hand under her jumper – only to withdraw it quickly as her mouth went limp, reminding me of the one-month moratorium. 'Don't worry,' Nusi said, 'I prepared myself when I put on my blouse.' She slid forward and lay back on the ground. 'I just wanted to find out if you liked me well enough to stick around for a month without it.' When I entered her, her body contracted as if she had been broken in two, and she enjoyed herself intensely. But as she brushed the leaves from her jumper, she remarked with a grimace: 'I was making love behind the bushes when I was seventeen – now I'm thirty-one, and I still have to do it behind the bushes. I'm making great progress, aren't I?'

She had been faithful to her husband until the last couple of years, when she had got friendly with a few men. 'But it never worked out. Men don't understand that if you have children, you can't just come running whenever they want you to. At least they said they couldn't understand – it was a good excuse to break off.'

I saw Nusi home in a taxi and the next day, Sunday, we met again. She told me she had dropped out of school two years before matriculation, to get married, and I persuaded her to enrol in a night school for the fall term and get her diploma. We could now go to our apartment with books and notes. When my mother was out, we made love; when my mother was home, I helped Nusi with her studies. She changed a great deal, became younger, fuller and prettier, but she was still as sceptical as ever. 'You're doing all this just so you won't have to feel guilty when you leave me.'

I met her husband only once, at dinner-time in their kitchen, and although I knew him as 'the drunk', he was entirely sober. I was introduced as an instructor from the school. József looked at me knowingly, then at Nusi, before he sat down to eat. He was a handsome, muscular man of about thirty-five, and he looked tired.

'School! Don't make me laugh, Nusi. You'll never make it.'

'She's bright,' I remarked.

'Like my ass,' he stated with finality, and attacked his food.

I attempted a tone of casual comment. 'Maybe you're too stupid to realize how smart she is.'

His jaw slowed down but he went on eating. Nusi's face, though unmoved, acquired the air of a smile. The children stared at their plates and picked up their forks smartly.

'Are you a bachelor?' József asked later. I could tell from his voice that he'd figured out a comeback.

'Yes,' I answered warily.

'It's an easy life, eh? A hen today, a chick tomorrow, eh?'

'Some people call them women.' I detested him for picking on Nusi instead of me. But he knew he had us both; his jaw speeded up.

Nusi turned towards him with murder in her eyes. 'I don't think Mr Vajda's private life is any of your business.'

His wife's look held the full measure of his guilt, and he began to laugh nervously. 'What have I done? Can't a man carry on a little conversation in his own home?'

'*His* home!' the old lady commented.

He turned towards me again. 'That's how it is when you get married, pal – the hens gang up on you. Don't ever get married. What I wouldn't give to be a bachelor again! Free as a bird – there's nothing like it.'

Nusi's mother couldn't suppress another comment. 'I'd like to know who's a bachelor if not you! You certainly act like one. I haven't seen a jailbird yet as free as you are.'

József shook his head in exasperation. 'It's not the same, Mother, it's not the same.' He shrugged his shoulder, indicating that whatever I might have taken, it wasn't of any value to him.

'I'm not your mother. And as far as I'm concerned, you might as well move next door.'

'How could I? How could I walk out on Nusi?' He spoke to his mother-in-law, but he was looking at his wife, pitying her with a vengeance. 'I'd feel sorry for her – who'd look after her if I left?'

Nobody said another word and after dinner József got up.

'I'll be back,' he said ominously to Nusi and, motioning goodbye to me, went out.

'Going to his girl friend's,' the old lady muttered, 'and he says he isn't a bachelor.'

Nusi let go of her temper. 'Did you hear him? He's eating here because he feels sorry for me! He's feeling sorry for me!' She was furious. She beat her fists on the table and the plates gave a clinking sound as they shook. 'I wish there was a God, he'd punish him for that, if nothing else!' She pushed back her chair and began pacing the kitchen, turning around herself like a prisoner in a cell remembering that she's got a life-term. 'He's ruined my life and he makes it look as if he's doing me a favour!' She raised her arms to heaven, repeating over and over again: 'I wish there was a God!' When I tried to quiet her, she turned on me. 'I don't care whether you leave me or not, but don't you be around when you can't be nice to me any longer! That's the worst thing you can do to a woman.' Then, at last, she began to cry, and her back bent as if suddenly the whole weight of that crammed and windowless kitchen had descended on her. Little Nusi was watching from her grandmother's arms, fearful and hesitant. Finally she freed herself and walked slowly to her mother and, reaching no higher, embraced her around the knees.

The next day I rented a hotel room so that we could be alone at least for twenty-four hours. As I wanted and loved her, I could cheer her up quite easily, and we had many good days before the snow fell.

Then I began seeing the wife of a homosexual.

She was the mother of two small boys. Her husband never touched her after fathering his alibis, but he forbade her to have affairs, as this might have led people to suspect him. Like every dictatorship, the regime was very strict about human nature, punishing all excesses and deviations, and he didn't want to risk his job, which had a villa and a chauffeured car to go with it. To make sure that she did nothing to endanger his vulnerable position, he had his sister living with them, whose job it was never to let her sister-in-law out of her sight. A considerate father, he asked his sons every evening to tell him about their day: what were they doing, what was Mother doing, did they meet interesting people? An imposing and manly figure, he attended official receptions and parties with his wife, and never left her side. He was jealous of her and wasn't ashamed to show it. He smiled modestly when people called him the Hungarian Othello. 'I guess I'm an old-fashioned husband,' he used to say, half-apologetically, 'I'm madly in love with my wife.' His wife was a beautiful and strange woman.

I met Nusi less often and had to make an effort to appear enthusiastic and interested. She accused me of being listless and impatient with her, and we began to have scenes. Yet I couldn't take Nusi at her word and leave her as she had said I should when I couldn't be nice to her any longer. She was going to night school and doing well, and had a good chance of getting a secretarial job in a couple of years. This, as she had so shrewdly predicted, helped to assuage my guilt, but not so completely that I could bring myself to break with her. If there was ever a woman who had suffered enough disappointments and deprivation to last a lifetime, that woman was Nusi. Yet I couldn't have an erection out of a sense of guilt and obligation. There were times when I went to bed with her, after complicated arrangements, and ended up by excusing myself.

'There's no animal as mean as a man who no longer loves a woman,' I had once declared apropos of her husband, and now the description was beginning to fit me. The welcome escapade from the misery of marriage was shaping up this time into an entanglement no less miserable than the marriage itself.

Once I confessed my problem to my new lover, lamenting that I didn't know which would be worse for Nusi – if we broke off or carried on. 'My dear,' she observed with a sigh, 'it isn't a moral problem you've got there – it's a case of extreme conceit.'

A few days later I had a violent argument with Nusi. She accused me of being bored with her, and I protested that I loved her just as much as ever and our only problem was her suspicious nature. As she wouldn't believe me, I finally admitted that she was right and suggested that we should quit.

After a few moments of dark deliberation, she straightened her shoulders and looked through me with her huge eyes. 'Well, it ends just like I always thought it would. I wish some day somebody would surprise me.'

14 On Anxiety and Rebellion

The dread of life, the dread of oneself . . .
Søren Kierkegaard

More was lost at Mohács.
Old Hungarian saying

I would have to describe a great many unamorous experiences to explain why I left Hungary again, this time for good – and so soon after offering to die for her. It seems I loved my country as ardently as if she were a woman, and just as inconstantly.

As love is an emotional glimpse of eternity, one can't help half-believing that genuine love will last for ever. When it would not, as in my case it never did, I couldn't escape a sense of guilt about my inability to feel true and lasting emotions. This shame was surpassed in intensity only by my doubts as to whether my lover had ever really loved me, when she was the one who ended the affair. In this I'm like most of my sceptical contemporaries: since we no longer reproach ourselves for failing to conform to absolute ethical precepts, we beat ourselves with the stick of psychological insight. When it comes to love, we reject the distinction between moral and immoral for the distinction between 'genuine' and 'superficial'. We're too understanding to condemn our actions; we condemn our motives instead. Having freed ourselves from a code of behaviour, we submit to a code of motivation to achieve the sense of shame and anxiety that our elders acquired by less sophisticated means. We rejected their religious morality because it set man against his instincts, weighted him down with a burden of guilt for sins which were in fact the workings of natural laws. Yet we still atone for the creation: we think of ourselves as failures, rather than renounce our belief in the possibility of perfection. We hang on to the hope of eternal love by denying even its temporary validity. It's less painful to think 'I'm shallow', 'She's self-centred', 'We couldn't communicate', 'It was all just physical', than to accept the simple fact that love is a passing sensation, for reasons beyond our control and even beyond our personalities. But who can reassure himself with his own rationalizations? No argument can fill the void of a dead feeling – that reminder of the ultimate void, our final inconstancy. We're untrue even to life.

Which may be why we prefer to rest our minds on less ephemeral subjects than ourselves. Personally, I found it a great relief to contemplate anxiety on the abstract level, and earned my BA and MA by diligent study, with particular attention to Kierkegaard. I also worried a great deal about the misery of our nation.

I cannot begin to tell you how we hated the Russians! My students don't like me to talk about this because they think I'm really arguing for more nuclear missiles. I am not, I don't believe in them, but just the same it is a fact that the Russians are the big imperialists of today, and within their colonies they are the most loathsome rulers; not content with robbing and bossing the natives, they want to be loved as well. One of their detestable fancies at the time was the forced parade on November 7 every year to celebrate the glorious birth of the Soviet Union. It was usually a cold and windy day, but the Party got everybody out by the simple device of ordering people to march in groups from the place where they worked or studied, so that the personnel officers could mark those who didn't show up. I remember the parade in 1952, when the Department of Philosophy marched behind the Bureau of Statistics, and I watched one of the clerks – a short, middle-aged man with a face as blue as ink – struggling to hold up his huge wooden placard. Several times he almost tripped over the long handle, as he tried to keep the cardboard picture of Rákosi from buckling in the wind, and he kept falling back into our ranks. Then, without any warning, he stepped out of line and began to beat the placard against a lamp post. 'I'm fed up with that ugly mug!' he cried. 'Bald-headed gangster! The one day I could sleep in, and they drag us out on the streets!' He was banging the placard with the sudden strength of a madman, and actually broke the thing to pieces. 'He's a Russian stooge! You hear? He's a murderer!' Out of nowhere, in an instant, there were two men in the blue uniforms of the Security Police, grabbing the man by the arm on each side. As they led him away, he began to whimper in the voice of an old woman. 'It was too heavy, comrades, that was the only reason, believe me . . . it was too heavy.'

One can't witness many such scenes without a growing desire to turn the winds. Indeed, in the early 1950's the whole country was charged with a pre-revolutionary atmosphere, and both the population and the Security Police were growing increasingly restless. More and more people started quoting Petöfi's poem which sparked the revolution against the Habsburg Empire on March 15, 1848.

Get on your feet, Magyar, it's now or never!

The 1848 revolution was beaten by the Austrians with the help of Imperial Russia; Petöfi himself was cut down by Cossack cavalrymen on a battlefield in Transylvania (the eastern part of Hungary, now occupied by Rumania). Yet neither the memory of defeat nor the smallness of our carved-up country could reconcile us to being bound to the Soviet Union. After all, the Turks couldn't hold us, not even after Mohács.

Mohács is a code word that makes Hungarians smoulder with stubborn pride: it's a word for the deluge and life thereafter, the name of an ancient battle which left lasting scars and bitter glory. In 1526 at a small settlement called Mohács on the Danube south of Budapest, the invading

Turks annihilated the whole Hungarian army of horsemen and foot soldiers, and for the next one hundred and seventy-four years Hungary was a province of the Ottoman Empire. During this period nearly half the country's population, millions of people, perished of starvation or the plague or were carried off to the slave markets of North Africa. Yet the Ottoman Empire is no more and there is still a Hungary. As far as Hungarians are concerned, this is the most important fact about history and politics, and they learn it when they are still small children, long before they reach school age. I first heard about the disaster at Mohács and the eventual downfall of our mighty conquerors from the Franciscan fathers, who were later driven out of their monastery by the security police on orders from the Russians. But that did not make anyone forget about the mortality of empires.

As Lajos Kossuth, the leader of the 1848 revolution, used to say, Hungarians have a *historic personality* – that is, they think in historic terms, in centuries and millennia, to brace themselves against the deadly powers of the day. Not only can they look back on a thousand years of recorded history as a nation, but it has been very much the same story through all that time, so that even the dimwitted can remember it: it is a story of losing and enduring. The history of their defeats and survival is a kind of religion with them as with the Jews; their heads are full of calamities which failed to destroy them.

> *We have already been punished*
> *for our past and future sins*

says the national anthem, expressing the defiant self-pity which makes Hungarians such restless and rebellious subjects, no matter how often they are beaten. Their moments of triumph have been too few to sustain their pride, but they glory in the fact that they have outlasted the Tartar invasion (1241), the Turkish occupation (1526–1700), the Austrian occupation (1711–1918) and the German occupation (1944

−45). Citizens of great states tend to believe that victories are forever; Hungarians focus their minds on the decay of power, on the inevitable fall of the victors and the resurgence of the vanquished. Which is why few of us ever imagined that the Russians would be staying for good; the question was only when they would be leaving and how.

In short, we hated the Russians with too much confidence and too impatiently.

As in most countries which lack a free press and every other open expression of public sentiment, the universities were hotbeds of sedition. At our meetings we argued that Hungary would be better off free and independent: we demanded that there should be an end to arbitrary arrests and executions, that the Russians should pay for the wheat and uranium they were taking out of the country, that there should be no more foreign bases and troops on Hungarian soil, that there should be free elections. We protested against the predominance of spineless mediocrities in all the seats of power, and we vowed to eliminate poverty. We felt the eyes of a hopeful world upon us (as well as the eyes of the police) and we dreamed of the double glory of liberating our country and contributing to the fall of the Russian Empire – even if we were killed first.

There wasn't a single student at our meetings who didn't recall the precedent set by Count Zrinyi in 1566. Count Miklós Zrinyi held out for years against the Turks in his small castle at Szigetvár until, finally, in 1566 Suleiman the Magnificent himself decided to crush him with an army of a hundred thousand strong. Zrinyi and his followers withstood this huge army for weeks, and when they had run out of food and ammunition, they dressed up in their parade uniforms, put gold coins in their pockets for the soldiers who would be men enough to kill them, and sprang forth from the ruins on a suicidal cavalry charge. They got quite far into the enemy camp before being cut down, and Suleiman the

Magnificent, shocked by the unexpected assault, and already suffering from acute aggravation at being held up for so long in front of an 'anthill', collapsed and died of apoplexy during the commotion around his tent. The resulting struggle for power among the Turkish moguls gave the Hungarians several years' respite. Moreover, not only did Count Zrinyi contrive to be defeated with spectacular success, but his great-grandson wrote a valiant epic poem about it, so that ever since then the old man has been leading his cavalry charge in the imagination of every generation of Hungarians, challenging them to fight regardless of the odds, demonstrating that even the few can inflict deadly blows on the many.

And we had all heard Hunyadi's bells ringing at noon. János Hunyadi was a 15th century *condottiere* who made himself the richest baron in Hungary and the general of a well-paid, well-trained army which wiped out the Turks in 1456 at the southern Hungarian capital of Nándorfehérvár (now called Belgrade), thereby saving Austria and Italy from what had appeared to be certain conquest by the forces of Islam. To commemorate Hunyadi's great victory over the infidels, Pope Calixtus III ordered the bells to be rung at noon till Judgment Day – which is why the bells still toll at midday in Catholic churches. Hunyadi's true victory of course was not over the Turks but over time: the way he set the bells ringing and kept us from despair. Dictatorship is a continuous lecture instructing you that your feelings, your thoughts and desires are of no account, that you are a nobody and must live as other people decide for you. A foreign dictatorship teaches you despair twice over; neither you nor your nation are of any consequence. But Hunyadi's bells were telling us otherwise, demonstrating the immense scope of historic action: win or lose, it was possible to do things which would keep our descendants from despairing hundreds of years hence.

The past had as much to do with our revolution as the

present. It shaped our dreams and our characters; the Hunyadis were like living relatives, people to live up to. The *condottiere*'s son Mátyás became a great Renaissance ruler, Matthias Corvinus (1458–90), patron of arts and letters, protector of the people, the first king to free the serfs and tax the nobles instead of the peasantry, hero of melodious poems and folk songs who made a habit of going about in peasant's clothes, so that the high and mighty could never be sure that the poor man they were about to ill-treat was not the king himself. Indeed, it was Mátyás's notion that every Hungarian was something of a king, and to this day most Hungarians suffer from princely conceit, though it goes together with a certain hardy notion of royalty. The man we most often saw depicted on a throne was György Dózsa, who was crowned (1514) on a white-hot iron throne with a white-hot iron crown – a peasant king roasted alive by the victorious aristocrats for raising a revolt in defence of the rights granted to the peasantry by the Hunyadis.

Hungarian history was rich in crimes inspired by greed and love of property; yet when fearing for our comfort, we had heroes who inspired us to risk not only our lives but also our possessions. First among these was Ferenc Rákoczi, who was born to estates that amounted to something like a fifth of Hungary, and in his time was one of the richest aristocrats in Europe. Prince Rákoczi (son of the ruler of Transylvania and a Zrinyi girl, herself a formidable general) risked everything to lead a war of liberation against Austria (1703–11), and in the end chose to give up his lands and spend the rest of his life in exile rather than submit to the Habsburgs. 'God can dispose of me in any way He pleases,' said Lajos Kossuth in 1848, echoing Rakoczi's sentiments, 'God can make me suffer, He can make me drink hemlock or send me into exile. But there is one thing not even God can do. He cannot make me an Austrian subject.'

It was not possible to make willing slaves of people who

had such ancestors to think about. And as we identified ourselves with our past heroes, so we all identified our oppressors with the oppressors of our ancestors. They were all one and the same lot, foreigners trying to lord it over us. Thus the Habsburgs were hated and resisted not only on their own account, but also on account of the Tartars and the Turks, and the Russians were detested not only on their own account, but also on account of the Tartars, the Turks, the Austrians and the Germans.

All the issues were clear, but when our demonstrations turned into a revolution in October, 1956, everything became blurred again. I fought like the others, but I was too terrified under the barrage of tanks and heavy artillery to feel heroic. If anything, I felt the curse of the lucky, among comrades lying on the pavement, dead but still bleeding. Nor could I feel a sense of righteousness: fighting against Russian occupation and a vicious and incompetent dictatorship, I found myself shooting at bewildered Ukrainian peasant boys who had as much reason to hate what we fought as we had. I thought I knew about wars from 1944, but it was an embittering shock to find that one can't confront the real enemy even in a revolution. Still I hung on through three weeks of street battles, hopping from ruin to ruin, scared and hungry – convinced after a while that we could neither win nor survive. But Zrinyi and Dózsa kept me on my feet. There were moments when I experienced a kind of mystic communion with my homeland, when I felt glad that, if I could do nothing more, at least I could join all those who had died for Hungary through a millennium of glory and ill luck. At twenty-three, I still believed that there could only be one true country for each man.

I turned into a philandering internationalist during my second crossing of the Austro-Hungarian border. There I was, fleeing again, with just a few other refugees this time, but on an equally cold December day, and through the same mountains. I had in fact the weird sensation of re-enacting an episode from my childhood. The sky was just as bleak as in the winter of '44; the quiet trees still stood tall, graceful and unperturbed, as if belonging to another world; and the snowy rocks echoed the machine-gun rattle as if the shooting hadn't stopped since I was a boy. This time we didn't need to fear the stray bullets of opposing armies: the unseen border patrol was aiming straight at us. I was less scared than enraged, realizing that I would be a hunted animal only so long as there was native soil beneath me. 'That's it!' I began to mutter to myself. 'So long, Hungary!' Wondering whether the bullets had hit the ground or my body as they hissed into silence, I tried to crawl under the snow and then run exposed – my passion for Hungary spent.

On the Austrian side of the border we found a road, and a passing milk truck picked us up and drove to the nearest village. The village square was already crowded with refugees, who were stamping their feet against the cold and staring at a line of brand-new silver buses. These had yellow, hand-painted signs proclaiming the points of their destination: Switzerland, USA, Belgium, Sweden, England, Australia, France, Italy, New Zealand, Brazil, Spain, Canada, West Germany and, simply, Wien. At the police station on the other side of the square, Red Cross officials were dispensing the first aid of hot coffee and sandwiches, while nurses in black coats and white caps scurried through the crowd in search of the wounded and babies in need. Other officials, appearing less sympathetic, were prodding the refugees to pick a bus and get on it.

We were bewildered by the sight of that muddy village square with its buses going to the four corners of the earth. Less than an hour before, we couldn't move without being shot at; now we were invited to choose our place under the sun. It didn't make sense to the senses, things didn't connect.

'There isn't enough transport here for all these people!' an elderly lady cried out in a sudden fit of hysteria. 'They'll overload the buses and we'll all get killed on these winding mountain roads!' Nobody laughed. Life had already manifested too many possibilities to make anyone feel confident.

'That bus over there marked Brazil – are they planning to drive it across the ocean?' I asked a round-faced girl who stood beside me in the crowd, looking frightened. She laughed nervously and explained that the buses went only as far as the various railway stations and refugee camps, where we would have to wait for screening and further transportation.

Where to spend the rest of one's life? A couple with a small baby, who had already boarded the bus for Belgium, got off and rushed to the vehicle marked New Zealand. There were others who walked up and down the lines of buses, reading and re-reading the names of countries with studious expressions, but without being able to make up their minds. And where was I finally going to get my PhD? In what language? It was impossible to believe that by taking a few steps in this or that direction I would settle these questions for good. I happened to be standing beside the yellow letters 'Sweden'. If I stepped on that bus, I would meet women in Stockholm and we'd fall in love – but if I moved on to the next vehicle, we'd never even learn of each other's existence. The round-faced girl finally made up her mind to go to Brazil. I saw her to her bus and before she stepped on – more to comfort my own helplessness than to cheer hers – I held her back and kissed her. She returned the kiss, and for a long moment we reminded each other that we were still a man and a woman, and that there would be men and women everywhere. I thought of asking her name, but I just put my hand where her breasts pushed forward her overcoat, and then watched her go. She found a seat by the window and smiled down at me, exposing a broken front tooth. If it hadn't been for that tooth, I might be writing these recollections in Portuguese. But the feel of her overcoat still warmed my fingers as I walked, no longer feeling quite so lost, to the bus marked 'Italy'. After weeks in the cold, I longed for the freedom of the sun.

The next day I was in Rome, in the company of three hundred other shaken-up Hungarians, none of whom I'd ever met before. Arriving at the new railway station, we saw people sipping their espresso at tables covered with white cloths, right beside the tracks. Only electric trains were running, and the shiny and spotless station looked like a pleasure palace, with the sun pouring in through the glass walls. We boarded buses again and were taken to the Albergo Ballestrazzi, an old and comfortable hotel on a narrow side-street off the Via Veneto. We found it difficult to get into the building: the way was blocked by trucks carrying gifts and by hundreds of people who had come to look at the *poveri rifugiati*. As I fought my way in, an elderly gentlemen pressed into my hand a bundle of banknotes (eighty thousand lire, I discovered when I counted them later). I was amazed to see pity on his face. Why should he pity me, I wondered, but then I caught myself and tried not to think of an answer. I thanked him in Latin and walked into the hotel. The lobby looked like a department store – compliments of the merchants of Rome. Racks of expensive suits, dresses and coats, tables covered with shirts, blouses, shoes – all that one could wish for when arriving in a strange city without luggage. However, as I joined my compatriots descending upon the goods, I heard a woman complaining loudly that there were no white kid gloves to fit her. I grabbed a big suitcase first and, carefully checking sizes and styles, selected six white shirts, ties, underwear, socks, two pairs of shoes, three suits, six black pullovers and a smart overcoat. The presents helped to delay the full realization that we had got away from everyone and every-thing we understood, cared for, hated or loved. We clutched our new possessions; and our faces, which had appeared so humble and fearful on the train, acquired the anxiously smug look of proprietors. Struggling through the crowd with my spoils, I noticed a thin, dark bellboy staring at me with contempt and revulsion. There I was, a foreigner, picking the best of everything for nothing. Had anyone ever asked him what *he* could use? I felt guilty and, at the same time, was overcome with a cosy sense of satisfaction at my own good luck.

We were each given a handsomely furnished private room, without charge, we were showered with all sorts of gifts and a great deal of cash, and we had nothing to do but relax and enjoy ourselves – and wait for the next drastic change in our fortunes.

After lunch on the second day, the student rebels at the Albergo Ballestrazzi were asked to come to the lobby to meet a journalist who was writing a series of articles about university life in Hungary. By then the lobby had regained its customary appearance, which was that of an inexplicably large drawing room in a modest middle-class home: dull mirrors in thick wooden frames, a threadbare carpet, and a great many old armchairs with their upholstery fading away. There was a woman settled comfortably in one of the chairs. She didn't seem to notice our small group approaching, although at the last moment she got up to greet us, shaking our hands briskly and repeating her first name.

'Paola.'

Paola was a most unlikely Italian: a straight-faced beauty, tall, blonde, and, as we were soon to learn, unsympathetic. Since none of us spoke Italian, she asked whether anyone could interpret for her in English. I offered my services, and she looked at me sceptically for a moment. 'All right,' she decided, 'let's get down to work.' First she wanted to know our academic qualifications, and what we had seen and done during the revolution. Whether we tried to tell a joke or tried to describe a tragic episode from the days of the fighting, she reacted only with her ball-point pen and showed no emotion except occasional anxiety that she wouldn't be able to read back her notes.

'That bitch hates our guts!' one of the boys complained. 'I'll be damned if I'll answer any more of her questions!'

'What did he say?' asked Paola, as I didn't translate.

'He's worrying whether we can tell you anything interesting enough to put into your articles.'

Paola raised her eyebrows but didn't comment. Finally she closed her notebook, announced that she would be back the next day, and concluded the interview on a personal note. 'I think you were all extremely lucky to get away safe and sound.'

Later that afternoon—I'd felt it coming on for days—I came down with a severe case of self-pity. I've been periodically subjected to this illness ever since childhood—in fact, I never recovered from it completely, only learned to live with it. However, this time the attack was more violent than ever before. I went up to my room and locked the door, and even ignored the bells for dinner: I couldn't have endured seeing and talking to anybody. Lying on my bed, I cried over my loneliness.

But why lie? I cried for my mother. I cried for a long time, shivering, feeling cast out of the womb of her protective love. I remembered my first year at school, how I used to run home, terrified that she wouldn't be there—she hadn't waited for me—she had run away! I remembered the day I cut my knee playing football and how it felt cured as soon as she began to bandage it. I could even taste the pancakes she made afterwards to cheer me. Now I hurt and I knew I could never run home again.

Soon I began to hate myself. Now there are times when I feel proud of having been able to fight for weeks in spite of being scared, but then I could only think that in the end I had run away. Who was I to try to tell Paola about Hunyadi and all the rest of them? Last week I was in Budapest, today I was in Rome—where would I be tomorrow, and what on earth for? I'd left my country, my lovers, my friends, my relations, and I'd never see them again. I couldn't comprehend what had possessed me to do it. Talking to that snob Italian journalist about the revolution, I persuaded myself that I no longer cared about Hungarian independence, liberty, equality and justice—all those things for which I'd irrevocably messed up my life. Even translating news about Hungary irritated me: I found my fellow refugees as tiresome and unnerving as the relatives of a former girl friend, and I resolved to keep away from them as much as possible. Lying on top of the bed all night with my clothes on, I slept little, and when I did I dreamed about a tank driving back and forth over me, flattening my body as thin as paper on the pavement.

The next morning I woke with a slight fever and a large, sore boil under my right armpit, and rushed off to the hotel doctor. According to him, my body was simply adjusting itself to the change of climate and diet; more likely it was rebelling against all the changes it had been subjected to. Both the fever and the boil continued to plague me for over a month, while I dragged myself through the museums and churches of Rome, either alone or in the company of Italians who had volunteered as escorts and guides for the refugees. They were kind, but they didn't know my name; if they knew it they couldn't pronounce it, and in any case I no longer knew whom it meant. I was just another *povero ungherese*. Within a couple of weeks I could get along in Italian, but I couldn't ignore the fact that I wasn't so much acquiring a new language as giving up my mother tongue. I had the ability to make contact with new people and places, but that talent obviously made me readier to abandon whatever I already had. I had even abandoned many of my interests: writing poetry, playing the piano. I could never stick to anything. Rome tempts one to reflect upon the past, and I began counting all the friends and lovers whom I had left, and all those who had left me. They appeared and disappeared: my whole life was a series of fade-ins and fade-outs. It seemed, in fact, that I had never gained anything I hadn't lost. I felt particularly guilty about Maya, and what troubled me most wasn't so much the fact that I made love with her cousin, but that I did it right there on Maya's bed – on the bed where she had taught me to love – a detail which I'd never thought much about, but which now struck me as a crime.

Incidentally, I must disagree with the great philosophers who urge us to Know Ourselves. Through all these days of penetrating self-analysis, I actually became meaner and stupider, out of sheer frustration. Every evening I withdrew early to my room to nurse my boil, wishing I'd been shot dead at the border. And every night, I had nightmares.

15 On Happiness with a Frigid Woman

I love you very much because with you
I found a way to love myself again.
Attila József

I was so sick of myself that I became attracted to a woman who showed absolutely no sympathy for me. Although Paola was writing an apparently endless series of articles about Hungarian students, her personal indifference to us wasn't affected by exposure to our company day after day. As I interpreted for her every afternoon in the dim lobby of the Albergo Ballestrazzi, I tried to guess her age. It could have been anywhere between twenty-eight and thirty-six: there were fine lines on her forehead and neck, yet her pale blue eyes shone with the unperturbed innocence (or ignorance?) of a young girl. When she walked into the lobby, wearing some clinging silk or knitted dress, strikingly elegant, her body looked as if it had been massaged into perfect shape by a long line of ardent lovers. But as she came closer, the warm glow turned into cold grace. She had a slim, distant face, the pale oval of a Byzantine madonna, and I began to wonder whether she would come to life if I touched her.

'You know,' I said to her one day, 'I'm really quite an experienced interpreter. I did a lot of it when I was a small boy.' I hoped, of course, that she would ask me where and why. At times when I didn't believe in myself, I used to exploit my American Army camp stories quite shamelessly as feelers and stimulants. But Paola wasn't interested. I also tried to impress her with my talent for languages, switching from English to Italian whenever I could, to show off each new word I had learned. She didn't react. Most of the boys excused themselves from her company as quickly as they could, and I was often left alone with her before she'd found out all she needed to know for the following day's instalment. I tried to help her, although my boil was throbbing and my whole body shivering with fever, and sometimes I alluded to my sufferings. She received such personal remarks with a raised eyebrow, as if I'd asked her to write a front-page story about my state of health.

'I'm sorry, but I'm afraid I'll have to leave you too,' I told her one day, thoroughly fed up, and in plain English. 'I feel so sick, I think I must be dying.'

'Now, try to say that in Italian,' she urged, in Italian. 'You shouldn't be so lazy – you should practise the language you know the least.'

Too weak to grind my teeth, I repeated in humble Italian that I was dying.

'Excellent!' Paola exclaimed, and actually smiled. 'See you tomorrow then.'

Infuriated, I went for a walk to calm myself. At the end of the Via Veneto stands one of the gates to the Villa Borghese, which is set in a luxuriant yet ordered park of ancient trees and fresh flowers, wild nature in a frame of carefully detailed artistic design, as much a forest as a garden. There is a small lake, there are exquisite paths winding past white marble statues, and everywhere (as the park occupies one of the Seven Hills of Rome) it offers glimpses of church domes, palace walls – a breath of the Renaissance. I'd never seen anything so magnificent and yet so soothing as the Borghese Gardens, and as I walked around I became sufficiently relaxed to realize that the fresh air and exercise had cleared my head and cooled my fever. Yet if it hadn't been for Paola's outrageous indifference to my sufferings, I would have spent the afternoon brooding in the hotel. Indeed, this sort of cause and effect turned out to be the pattern of our relationship: Paola used to make me furious, but I ended by feeling healthier and brighter afterwards.

'I'm not an outgoing personality,' she observed after our last interview in the lobby, when we were left by ourselves again. 'And I concentrate on what I'm doing. I noticed your friends don't like me.'

'They think you're humourless, bloodless and insensitive,' I informed her.

'That sounds pretty astute.' She was impressed, as if we were talking about someone else. 'I must say, I was favourably impressed by most of you,' she added in the spirit of objectivity. 'You're all too wrought up about politics, but at least you're not like Italian men – you're not obsessed with sex.'

I don't know how the other boys would have reacted if they'd been present to hear the compliment, but its effect on me was profound. Once when I was in hospital at the age of nine with a ruptured appendix, I heard the doctor advising my mother to make arrangements for my funeral, and I was back on my feet in two weeks. Paola's remark affected me the same way. I asked her whether she would show me around Rome, in return for my services as an interpreter; she agreed, and we made an appointment for the following day. After she left I went up to my room, did ten push-ups, had a bath, and resolved to make love with that woman as soon as my boil disappeared.

It was on our second date, about the middle of January, that I began to make verbal passes at my guide. She was leading me through a small museum, and I kept insisting that she was more beautiful than any of the paintings or statues she pointed out to me. In her reddish-brown dress, with her blonde hair combed sleekly upward from her slim, impassive face, she looked like a royal Egyptian mummy, enamelled in russet and ochre – whatever period she conjured up, it was never the present. She didn't acknowledge my flattery, except by raising her eyebrows. Was it a childhood habit of hers, I wondered, to express surprise and disapproval in this way? Had she tried for years to get rid of the habit, and finally given up in despair? I imagined everything I could that might have made her more human and likeable.

When we were about to part, in front of the museum, I tried my luck.

'Do you know, I've never been invited for a meal in an Italian home?'

'You haven't missed anything – the hotels have the best food in Rome.'

'Still, it's not the same as a home-cooked meal.'

'What's got into you today? For one thing, I'm married. For another, if I want to have you for dinner, I'll ask you.'

That was definite. I held out my hand. 'Well, it was nice knowing you, maybe we'll meet again if I stay in Italy.'

Paola took my hand, but didn't let it go. Some women shouldn't be rude, if they don't want to end up being kind, out of uneasiness over their bad manners. 'I suppose if I don't invite you for dinner you'll think it's because you're a refugee.'

'Not at all,' I protested, pressing her long, smooth fingers. 'I realize it's simply because you don't like me personally.'

She withdrew her hand and looked around to see whether any of the passers-by were watching us. 'I've nothing at home but canned food.'

'I love canned food.'

She narrowed her eyes this time, though it may have been on account of the sharp sun. 'All right, but remember – you asked for it.'

As Paola led me into her apartment, I kissed the back of her neck. Her skin was so fair that it seemed to radiate light in the windowless alcove. She stood still for a moment, then removed her body and the smell of her perfume to a bright, modern kitchen.

'I'd be the wrong woman for you,' she said firmly, 'even for a casual affair.'

Still, our situation was becoming more intimate. She heated up some canned ravioli and we sat down at the kitchen table to an uninspired meal, just like an old married couple. Which reminded me that Paola had said she was married. 'Where is your husband?' I asked anxiously. I'd quite forgotten about him.

'We haven't been living together for the past six years,' she admitted with an apologetic half-smile. 'We're legally separated – that's what we have in Italy instead of divorces.'

'Why did you leave him?'

'He left me.'

The answer didn't invite further questions, and it was just as well, for had Paola told me more I would probably have lost my nerve and retreated to the Albergo Ballestrazzi. We began to talk about politics and she explained to me the differences between the various factions of the ruling Christian Democratic Party, in a relaxed manner, as if she'd taken for granted that I understood that all I was going to get was canned food. Inspired both by piqued pride and by the smell of her perfume (I'd somehow been unaware of it on other occasions, though now it overpowered even the ravioli), I could hardly wait for the end of the meal, and I declined her offer to make coffee, as it would have involved an intolerable waste of time. I asked her to show me the apartment, but it impressed me only as a blue and green background to her figure, until we came to a huge round bed. Paola let me kiss and hold her, without responding; but when I began to unbutton her dress, she tried to push me away with her elbows and knees. The tight dress frustrated her efforts as much as I did, and at last I succeeded in releasing her breasts, which swelled up as they emerged from the brassière. Neither of us had spoken, but when my head bent over her white bosom she remarked, with a tinge of malice in her voice, 'I'm frigid, you know.'

What was I to do, standing against her, with her bare breasts cupped in my hands? 'I've just come from a revolution,' I declared manfully, but without showing my face, 'you can't scare me.'

At that Paola raised my head and gave me a strong, passionate kiss. While we were undressing each other, I began to hope that this mysterious Italian woman had been lying to test me. Hadn't Nusi warned me that she wouldn't sleep with me for at least a month, not an hour before we first made love?

Unfortunately, there are few happy parallels in life. When we had got rid of our clothes, Paola gathered hers together, piled them neatly on the bureau, and hung her dress in the closet. Then she went to the bathroom to brush her teeth. I watched her with a mixture of disbelief, fear, and longing. Naked, her buttocks were larger than they had seemed under the dress, but they only gave an exciting, firm centre to her tall, slim body. As she turned from the washbasin, the combination of her long blonde hair and the short blonde tuft between her thighs brought back the painful cramps of my boyhood. But she walked towards me, in the glorious strangeness of her naked body, as casually and deliberately as if we'd been married for ten years. She stuck out the tip of her tongue – then walked right past me to take off the bedspread, which she folded three times and deposited on the chair. Terrified that she would spend the whole night puttering about like this, I grabbed her by her cool buttocks.

'They're too big,' she commented soberly.

I squeezed them with the violence of my frustration and it must have hurt, for she bled me in turn, sinking her teeth into my tongue. Only the fact that I'd been without a woman for over two months enabled me to get through the next quarter of an hour. Paola behaved more like a considerate hostess than a lover: she raised and twisted her body so attentively that I felt like a guest for whom so much is done that he can't help knowing that he's expected to leave soon. I didn't feel at home in her, and couldn't come for a long time. At the end, I ran my hands over her body, still not quite believing that there could be such perfect form without content.

'Did you enjoy it?' she asked.

As all else had failed, I tried to soften her with words. 'It was wonderful.'

'Oh, I'm glad, glad, glad.'

'I love you.'

'Don't talk like that,' Paola protested. She pulled the blanket up to her neck, preventing me from hovering over her body. 'You make me feel I should tell you the same thing. And I can't say I love you. It wouldn't be true.'

'Let's lie then!'

'Maybe you can lie, but I can't.'

While thinking out some polite way of leaving, I reached down between her legs and began playing with her, almost mechanically—only to discover that she liked this better than our lovemaking.

'Aren't we having a good time without making things up?' she asked comfortably.

Was she one of those women who could only come in a roundabout way? Never one to leave well enough alone, I hopefully pulled off the blanket and turned myself around to reach the source of her mystery. But she pushed my head away and shoved me violently in the chest, almost rolling me off the bed. 'Don't! It's unclean to do a thing like that.'

'But you're clean. You smell so good!'

'I'm not a pervert—I like it the normal way.'

'You mean, when you don't come?'

'I'd be ashamed.'

'Do you know,' I told her, 'one of the most common endearments in Hungarian is *my sweet flesh*. Nobody is ashamed to say it. Lovers call each other *my sweet flesh* in front of everybody.'

'You would be disgusted.'

I tried to persuade Paola that she was perfect in all her

parts, but she was stubborn. The more we talked about it, the less it mattered. Finally, I looked around for my clothes on the grey broadloom—it was getting dark—then got up and began to dress.

'Why are you getting dressed?' she asked, annoyed.

'I think I should be going—it's getting late.'

Paola was silent for a while, then burst out unexpectedly, 'You men are all vain monkeys. You don't enjoy women, you don't even enjoy your own orgasm. The only thing you really want is to make a woman go off with a big bang. It had to be men who invented the atomic bomb.'

'Maybe you'd have a bang, if you'd only try.'

'Oh, God, I'm thirty-six years old, Andrea. I've tried enough.'

I turned on the light to find my shoes.

'Did I tell you about my husband?' she asked, propping herself up on her elbow. 'He's a lawyer—he ran for Parliament twice on the Monarchist ticket, and was defeated, of course. He thought he lost because I was frigid. I had destroyed his self-confidence. He read a lot on psychoanalysis and decided that I must be a masochist, so he took to beating me with a wet towel every time we made love. I got so sick of that towel, I finally told him maybe we should find out whether I was a sadist.'

'What did he say?'

'He actually wanted to try it. I did hit him one evening, he insisted, but I didn't enjoy that either, in fact I hated it. So I said there'd be no more experiments.'

I sat down on the edge of the bed to tie my shoelaces. 'None of your lovers were any better?'

'Oh, it's always on the basis of friendship. There's an editor on the paper, he comes up sometimes. But he doesn't want to mess around like you do. He's fifty-one.' I hated the idea of trespassing on an elderly gentleman's territory, and it must have showed. 'What are you thinking about?' she asked, reaching out to brush my hand affectionately. A most contrary woman.

'I was wondering what's going to happen when the Italian government gets tired of keeping us in the hotel,' I lied. But when I'd said the words I did begin to fret again about what was going to become of me. 'The worst of it is, I really don't have the faintest clue. I got a list of Italian universities from the Red Cross and sent off a bunch of applications – but even if they accept my degrees here, they probably won't let me teach, with my Italian. And I want to be a teacher, I've been preparing for it too long to give it up now.' I already saw myself as a waiter in a cheap café, taking small tips.

'Oh, you'll get something. And in the meantime, you're in Rome, staying in a hotel that would cost you ten thousand lire a day if you had to pay for it. Why don't you just relax and enjoy yourself? I noticed you're awfully tense.'

How would I be otherwise, in her company? 'It's easy for you to talk,' I complained bitterly. 'You have a steady job, you're in your own country, you don't have to worry what'll happen to you tomorrow.'

Paola got up and began to dress. 'Nobody knows what'll happen to him tomorrow. You like to feel sorry for yourself.' Now that we were discussing a problem that she could handle with pure reason, she regained her confident manner. And she must have felt relieved, as I did, that we both had our clothes on again: it was certainly more appropriate to the nature of our relationship. 'A lot of people,' she added briskly, 'would commit murder to have your problems.'

'I shouldn't be talking to you, you only remind me that I'm absolutely alone in this world.'

'Who isn't?'

For some reason – perhaps because she went back to the bathroom to comb her hair, with slow dreamy movements of her arm, as if we'd had a great time – I felt compelled to convince her that I had every reason to feel rotten. I'd made my whole past simply irrelevant by leaving Hungary, didn't she understand that? Nothing I'd done in my life meant anything any more. I told her about the Russian tank which drove over me every night.

'Because you keep brooding over what you've been through. You spend all your time feeling sorry for yourself.'

'I wouldn't dare in your presence.'

'You're a student of philosophy – you should know that life is chaotic, senseless and painful most of the time.'

'That's exactly why I'm so miserable,' I protested.

'At twenty-three, aren't you too old to get upset about such obvious things?'

I tried to prove that I knew more about the absurdity of existence than she did, and we began to argue about Camus and Sartre. While we talked I wandered from room to room, so as not to be too close to that mean woman. When would I have an apartment like hers, I wondered. It was a truly extraordinary place. There was none of the oppressive stinginess of most modern apartments about it, although the building was only a few years old. The ceilings were high, the rooms enormous, and they had the most exciting layout. The bedroom was round and had a big semi-circular window, at which stood a half-moon-shaped desk with a portable Olivetti on it. The only other furniture was the huge round bed, which Paola had quickly made up again with its gold quilted cover. The adjoining grey-marble and gilt bathroom was the size of a small public bath. The blue and green living room was shaped like a capital S, and this wavy line gave it an illusion of movement, in spite of the large and solid armchairs and sofas, which were made to fit the curves of the wall.

'I'm not surprised,' I told Paola, 'that you can accept the absurdity of existence with such equanimity.'

'I've had to move out of this place twice because I couldn't afford the rent. I haven't got a car.'

'Doesn't your husband pay you alimony?'

'Well, he's supposed to according to law, and he can certainly afford it, but I couldn't very well go to court and force him to support me, considering the miserable time I gave him.'

I wasn't inclined to contradict her. The time had come to say goodbye, but before I could introduce the subject of our parting, she put her arm through mine with a confident gesture. 'Let's go for a walk, Andrea.'

Did she think I planned to go on seeing her? When we were in the elevator, she drew my head to hers and whispered, 'You know, I enjoy it in my own little way. You make me feel like a real woman.' Which was Paola's best argument to convert me to a stoical view of life: instead of feeling sorry for myself, I began to feel sorry for her.

But I showed up on our next date mainly because I had received a letter from the Monsignor at the University of Padua. He informed me that Italian universities in general required more credits in Christian philosophy than I seemed to have; that at the moment they had no funds available to grant me a scholarship for the time I would require to perfect my Italian and complete my doctoral thesis; and that I should perhaps apply to the American foundations. The Monsignor also advised me, since I spoke German and English, to inquire at universities in West Germany and the English-speaking countries. It didn't sound as if Italy had any use for Signor Andrea Vajda with his *cum laude* degrees from the University of Budapest.

As I was reading and re-reading the letter, I had a sudden desire to hear Paola telling me that it was nothing to complain about, and that there were people starving to death in Sicily. Besides, I began to wonder about the fact that, in all her thirty-six years, no man had been able to get through to her. What if I could make all the difference? Back home in Budapest, I wouldn't have conceived such an ambition. By the time I recovered from my hopeless love for Ilona, I had learned that there were more important obstacles to overcome in this world than a difficult woman. As I began to take my studies seriously, I invested my ego in becoming a good teacher and, possibly, the author of a few worthwhile philo-sophical essays; and my masculine craving for excitement, conflict and danger was satisfied by the Security Police. Much as I loved women, all I wanted from them was straight affection, and I came to avoid those whose behaviour suggested complications. But in Rome, where I was fed, housed and bored, reduced to the uncertain and purpose-less life of the undisposed refugee, Paola offered the happi-ness of constant challenge.

We began to spend most evenings together – sometimes the night, in Paola's apartment. Being with her was like living on a high plateau. The air was clear but thinner, one had to slow down one's responses, breathe lightly, be cool and careful and avoid excitement. For obvious reasons, conversation was a very important element in our affair.

Once when we were in bed and I wanted to try a way which she found strange, Paola leaped out of bed and returned with a pile of books by and about Sartre. 'I've been thinking,' she said, 'you must be depressed with nothing to do here. You must work on something. You know, there's no reason why you shouldn't write your thesis, just because you don't know yet where you're going to submit it. And I can help you to get the journals and papers you need.' It was impossible not to see that Paola had brought me the books to evade a struggle on the bed, but this didn't make her suggestion any less appealing. We spent the rest of the evening poring over the books, and the next day I began to make notes on *Sartre's theory of self-deception as it applies to the body of his own philosophy*, for which the University of Toronto granted me a PhD three years later. It appeared in the second issue of *The Canadian Philosophical Review* (Volume 1, Number 2, pages 72–158) gaining me whatever standing I have in my profession. At any rate, thanks to Paola's way of evading our most personal problem, I became involved in something I enjoyed doing and thought useful –

which did a great deal to steady my nerves. I stopped having nightmares, and began to fit into the world again.

However, the novelty of my spiritual well-being wore off after a while. No longer starved for either sex or companionship, I missed increasingly what Paola couldn't give, and began to lose hope of ever changing her. At the beginning we used to leave the lights on in her bedroom, but we gradually got into the habit of turning off all the switches before touching each other. I was especially incensed by her violent throes and sighs. As she grew fond of me, she wanted to show that I made her enjoy herself in her own little way, but her pretences only served as incessant reminders that she was having an indifferent time and going to the trouble of acting for it. I was bitterly conscious of being a joy-parasite, a sexual free-loader. All of which made me obsessed with her stubborn vagina, that pine-smelling fountainhead of our predicament. I often tried to kiss it, but she always pushed me away. If I argued, she became desolate.

'I was happy as long as I was a virgin,' she once complained bitterly. 'Then it was enough that I was a good-looking, intelligent, nice girl. Ever since, it's always the same story. What a sexy-looking woman, let's lay her. And when she finally gives in, sick to death of being pestered, what a big disappointment! I wish I were ugly, then everybody'd leave me alone and I wouldn't have to listen to complaints.'

'Who's complaining? Don't talk nonsense.'

'You wanted canned food, remember?'

We made love then the normal way, simulating enjoyment in unison. Our bed grew damp with the sweat of remorse, and there was nothing we could do about it. At first I thought she would welcome my attempts to give her joy, but she took them as an admission that I held it against her that she couldn't satisfy herself. Of course I tried to convince her that there was more to sex than pleasure – much more, indeed! – and that it was facile, idiotic, to make a fetish of orgasm. She agreed. But whatever is sanctioned by society as a principal good also becomes a moral imperative (whether it's the salvation of the soul or the body) and we can't fail to attain it except at the peril of our conscience. Paola couldn't help feeling guilty about her frigidity any more than she could have felt righteous about making love in the Middle Ages. In fact, I sometimes wished us back into the twelfth century, when her coldness would have been the pride of her virtue and she would have felt sinful only for the delights of the flesh, whereas now she was doomed to feel guilty for her painful frustration. Nor could I help sharing her guilt. If she had been younger and not yet convinced that her misfortune wasn't her lover's fault, we might have ended up strangling each other (even among frigid women, older women are preferable), but though we both knew I wasn't the cause, I was still accessory to her suffering. And my attempts to relieve it only made matters worse. On the other hand, to ignore the despairing excitement and let-down of her body would have meant denying even the bond of elementary sympathy between us. We were getting lost in a desert of impossibilities.

Paola said that I made her feel like a real woman by wanting and enjoying her, and at times she was the blissful mother of my pleasure. But the mistress couldn't have endured her smouldering expectations which never caught fire, except in a state of vigilant despair. There would be very few sexual problems if they could all be ascribed to inhibitions, yet at first I took it for granted that Paola refused to consent to any unfamiliar love-play out of modesty. However, her violent resistance showed not shyness but fear. It leaped through the blue of her eyes and hung over her long white body – the fear of false hopes and deeper defeats.

Even a sentimental glance put Paola on her guard. She had a horror of being carried away, or rather of forgetting that she couldn't be. On a mild evening late in March we sat at the edge of a sidewalk café, watching the flow of human splendour, and as Paola seemed relaxed and cheerful, I began to eye her as pleadingly as if she were a strange woman I was trying to pick up. She raised her eyebrows and turned her head away. 'Your trouble is that you love yourself too much.'

'How could you possibly love anybody, if you don't even love yourself?'

'Why should I love myself?' she asked with her casual and depressing objectivity. 'Why should we love anybody?'

We might have been able to cope with her lack of physical satisfaction, but the metaphysical consequences were opening a void between us. They made it difficult – in fact, for a long time impossible – to test my hopeful guess at an easy way to free us from the sting of her husband's wet towel.

Late one Saturday morning, I was awakened by the heat. The sun was shining into my eyes through the curved window panes and gauzy white curtains, and the temperature in the room must have been at least ninety degrees. During the night we had kicked off the blanket and the top sheet, and Paola was lying on her back with her legs drawn up, breathing without a sound. We never look so much at the mercy of our bodies, in the grip of our unconscious cells, as when we are asleep. With a loud heartbeat, I made up my mind that this time I would make or break us. Slowly I separated her limbs: a thief parting branches to steal his way into a garden. Behind the tuft of blond grass I could see her dark-pink bud, with its two long petals standing slightly apart as if they, too, felt the heat. They were particularly pretty, and I began smelling and licking them with my old avidity. Soon the petals grew softer and I could taste the sprinkles of welcome, though the body remained motionless. By then Paola must have been awake, but pretended not to be; she remained in that dreamy state in which we try to escape responsibility for whatever happens, by disclaiming both victory and defeat beforehand. It may have been ten minutes or half an hour later (time had dissolved into a smell of pine) that Paola's belly began to contract and let up and, shaking, she finally delivered us her joy, that offspring not even transient lovers can do without. When her cup ran over she drew me up by my arms and I could at last enter her with a clear conscience.

'You look smug,' were her first words when she focused her critical blue eyes again.

We had one friend in common: a Hungarian-Italian painter, Signor Bihari, a tall, sporty-looking gentleman in his sixties. He always wore an elegant ascot scarf of his own design, and used to assure everyone that his main ambition in life was to stay as young as Picasso. He had started his career as a reporter in Budapest, but his paper had sent him on a two-week assignment to Paris in 1924 and he hadn't been back in Hungary since. His wife was a French lady whom he used to drag along to the Albergo Ballestrazzi so that she could at least hear Hungarian conversation and find out how her husband's mother-tongue sounded. She would stand at his side, bewildered, while he talked with the refugees. Signor Bihari knew not only Paola but also the editor who'd been friendly with her, and it was thus I learned that Paola had broken off with the man, telling him that she was in love with a young Hungarian refugee.

I quoted the statement back to Paola, curious whether she would acknowledge such an affectionate confession.

'Don't you believe it,' Paola said. 'I wanted to get rid of the man peacefully, and you can't get rid of anybody by telling him the truth of the matter.'

'And what's the truth of the matter?'

We were in her kitchen and she was cooking dinner for us, wearing only a bra and a light skirt, for it was already summer. I sat by the kitchen table, smelled the delicious food and watched her moving about, with a stirring of all sorts of appetites.

'Well,' she said, her attention still on her steaming pots and pans, 'the truth of the matter is that in ten years or so

I'm going to quit working and retire to our old house in Ravenna. My parents'll probably be dead by then, and I'll live there with some old maid. Our noses will get sharper every winter, I suppose.'

'Maybe I'll be teaching in Ravenna.'

'There are enough philosophy teachers in Italy to fill the Adriatic. You'll emigrate to some other country sooner or later. Which will be just as well, because it'll save me from the unpleasant experience of having you get bored with me.'

Her prediction that I would get bored with her seemed most improbable. There was now less tension between us than with most of the women I'd ever known, and our relaxed happiness used to remind me of the bad times I'd experienced with all my other lovers. I remembered the moments of anxiety when I used to recite historical dates in my head while we were making love, so that I wouldn't enjoy myself too much and too quickly for my lover's convenience. With Paola, I had no reason to regulate my response. She used to receive me when already shaking and flowing – which somehow made her more desirable each time. We got along famously. We were happy.

But I couldn't get a job, and the Albergo Ballestrazzi was to be given back to paying guests at the beginning of August. If I went to live with Paola, she might have to support me for a very long time. So she turned out to be right about my leaving Italy. Signor Bihari had a friend at the Canadian Embassy who had friends in Toronto who promised me a job at the university there, and I didn't have the courage to refuse.

On August 16, Paola accompanied me to the airport. We were rocking in the back of an ancient taxi and, as I was gloomy and speechless, she pulled my hair.

'It isn't that you're sorry to leave me,' she said accusingly, 'you're scared of going to Canada.'

'Both,' I admitted, and began to cry, which I believe made

our parting easier for my unsentimental lover.

After we said good-bye at the gate of the runway, Paola turned to leave, then came back and gave me another hug.

'Don't worry, Andrea,' she said, quoting our private joke with a serious smile, 'every road leads to Rome.'

16 On Grown Women as Teenage Girls

Sex on the moon.
Norman Mailer

There is a new loneliness in the modern world: the solitude of speed. It is so easy to get on a plane and go to some place where you don't know anybody. I have no relatives in Ann Arbor: the ones I know about are in London, Frankfurt, Milan, Paris, Lyons and Sydney, Australia. My father's sister, Aunt Alice, an old lady now, is growing strawberries near Freiburg. A niece of mine who went to Barcelona married a Spanish engineer with whom she emigrated to Caracas. I have a half-black American cousin who is, or was when I last heard from her, a museum curator in Cleveland. An uncle of mine who worked in the space program at Cape Kennedy has retired to New York and lives on the Upper West Side. I myself came from Rome to Toronto – for good, as I thought – and here I am in Michigan. Your typical small-town American, who often misses the big-city life of Toronto.

I still remember the buzzing in my ears as I walked away from the plane on the concrete of a new continent, feeling as if my blood had dried up. A fat uniformed official gave me a blue slip which bore my name and the affirmation of my new existence: *landed immigrant*. He also handed me a five-dollar bill, explained that it was 'welcome money', and gave me a receipt to sign. Then he indicated with a wave of his hand that I could go anywhere I wanted. I would have liked to turn around and go straight back to Europe, but as I had only the receipt for my one-way ticket and less than a hundred dollars, including the welcome money, I dragged my three suitcases out of the dirty, run-down air terminal. After one glance at the vast, empty, alien landscape, I sought courage from my own giant shadow, which the sun cast ahead of me on the ground. A few miles away a huge malevolent cloud of brown smog hung in the air, signalling the presence of the city where I was to live.

My taxi-driver was a bulky man with a square, flat face and dull eyes, who didn't encourage conversation. But I knew no one else, so I told him I had just arrived in Canada and needed a cheap room in the university district. Luckily he turned out to be an Austrian, and when he learned that I came from Hungary and knew Salzburg well, he became friendly and promised to set me up. Talking into the rear-view mirror, he observed that I was young enough to be his son, and warned me that there were no coffee houses in Toronto and that I should get myself a girl friend as quickly as possible, because prostitutes were expensive. As we drove towards the city on the Queen Elizabeth Way, with tall poplars and banks of shrubs on either side, and then along the shores of Lake Ontario, I began to think the landscape was quite pleasant and not unlike the country around Lake Balaton. But the Austrian insisted that it was peopled with different spirits than the ones I knew back home.

'The natives are just as human as people any place else, but they won't admit it unless they're drunk. And then they pass out on the floor of the cab or get the bright idea to rob you. Sometimes I wish I was driving a carriage in Vienna in the days of old Franz Josef.' There was a brief pause to honour the passing of the Austro-Hungarian Empire, which neither of us could possibly have remembered. 'Canadians love money first, which is OK,' he went on, 'but then comes liquor, then TV, hockey, then food. Sex is way down on the list. When you'd grab a girl, a Canadian grabs another drink. The place is full of fat men and unhappy women.' He himself looked quite heavy, I remarked. 'Oh, well,' he conceded ominously, 'when you've lived here as many years as I have, you'll change too.'

We parked on Huron Street, a narrow tree-lined street of shabby, turreted, dark red brick Victorian mansions converted into rooming houses, and walked from door to door inquiring about rents. The Austrian upbraided half a dozen landladies for their exorbitant prices before advising me to take an attic room. It had a low, slanted ceiling, ornate wallpaper and a linoleum floor, but I was anxious to settle somewhere, if only temporarily. We went back to the car for my luggage, and I thanked him for his inexplicable kindness. 'Tomorrow I wouldn't bother with you,' he said, raising his open palms for emphasis, 'but I couldn't turn down a man on his first day in Canada. I came here alone myself – in '51, in the middle of winter! You never forget the first day, believe me. It's the worst.' He took the fare but wouldn't accept a tip, and we parted with an affectionate handshake.

I saw him again three years later: he had given up driving and had opened the Viennese Strudel Shop on Yonge Street. He must have been doing well, for the last time I saw him he told me he'd just come back from a holiday in Japan. Meeting him again as a successful small businessman and world traveller, still overweight, moody over his sudden affluence, reinforced my memory of him as an almost mystical guide to this continent of immigrants.

The things he warned me against, the things which I disliked today as much as on the day I arrived – drinking parties, hockey, television – are as conspicuous features of life in the United States as in Canada, but so is the willingness to give a break to a stranger. Thanks to Signor Bihari's friend at the Consulate in Rome, I met a number of academic officials who seemed to be looking forward to helping me. They got me a job at a boys' school for the first year, and then helped me to obtain a lectureship at the University of Toronto. After five years at U of T I came to The University of Michigan at Ann Arbor, where I remain to this day—though I am thinking of applying for a post at Columbia. I suspect it's impossible for some people to stay in one place for good, once they have left the scenes of their childhood; or it may be that however long I remain on this continent, I'll never feel quite at home, and that is why I want to move about. Still, I wish I lived in a town where the streets and squares were named after great men instead of developers, mayors or trees.

Why can't we have cities which honour genius at every corner? How could children grow up to be civilized citizens when they have never raced each other along Shakespeare Avenue? How could people aspire to anything but money when there is nothing in their surroundings to remind them of the immortals who created things which do not lose their value with inflation? I wrote letters to editors proposing, inter alia, to rename "M" streets after Molière, Mozart, or Mark Twain. But all this falls outside the scope of this memoir, except to suggest that if after all these years I still haven't adjusted to the New World, I must have been an extraordinarily bewildered person when I arrived from Rome.

It seemed at times, especially during my first couple of years in Toronto, that I had come over the Atlantic only to lose my cherished faith in older women. And at the risk of undermining my own argument, I must admit that there are women whose years have left marks only on their face, and none on their brain or character. In fact, it would appear that stupid girls grow more inane as they mature. They're consumed with vanity and avarice, which may be the reason why they spared me in my student days when I was young and poor. On the few occasions when I caught their attention back in Budapest, I knew how to recognize them and could escape in time. But knowing that I should keep my distance from women who adored Comrade Stalin or gypsy music was flimsy protection against similarly twisted personalities in North America. It took time to realize that I should stay clear of women who lower their glances with a blush of respect at the mention of the Bell Telephone Company, who watch television for hours every day, who hum tunes about detergents, who kiss with their eyes open and pride themselves on being practical. Such women are often dangerous and always painful, and I still resent my bad luck in running into one of them on my second day in the New World, at a time when it took very little to depress me in my strange new surroundings.

She appeared, appropriately enough, in a setting of movie magazines, *TV Guides*, milk shakes, toothpastes, medicines, cameras, scissors, Kleenex, and various Specially Reduced Items in a drugstore on Bloor Street. It was half a block away from my rooming house, and I'd gone there for an early supper, to avoid venturing any farther out into the city than I absolutely had to. I'd finished my meal and was drinking a glass of milk when I became aware of her smiling at me. I don't think I ever needed a smile or a look more than at that moment. Feeling all alone on an alien planet, not knowing a single soul, man or woman, whom I could call even for a chat, absolutely terrified by the prospect of returning to my dingy attic room on my own, I was suddenly transported back to earth, to sunshine. She was about thirty-five, with short, curly auburn hair, a heavy mouth and a plump but rather good figure, and she was smiling and looking directly into my eyes, not hiding her liking for me. I no longer felt thousands of miles from home.

When I got up to pay my bill she stepped outside and loitered by the door, eyeing me through the glass. I was hoping that she was a lonely divorcee, as much in need of a lover as I was, and I already saw us curled up together for the night. As I left the drugstore she was only a few paces ahead of me. 'Forgive me for speaking to you without an introduction,' I said as I caught up with her, 'but I would like to know you.'

'Go away!' she commanded in a voice heavy with outrage,

and began to walk faster.

Crazed with loneliness rather than desire, I kept up with her. 'My name is András,' I said. 'What's yours?'

'Leave me alone or I'll call the police.'

An old woman passing by heard her and gave me a nasty look. I stopped for a moment but then, remembering how she had smiled at me in the drugstore, I hurried after her, only to be threatened again.

'If you keep on pestering me, I'll scream for help. What are you, a rapist?'

I gave up, and watched her walk away. She looked back a couple of times to see whether I was following her; and the second time she turned around, she was laughing.

I was furious. It wasn't so much that she'd made a fool of me, but that she had no conceivable reason for doing so except pure impersonal malice. I'd known young girls who amused themselves with sadistic teasing, but a woman who couldn't have been a day younger than thirty-five yet behaved like a frustrated teenage girl was a novel experience. I'm superstitious about bad starts, and the incident filled me with foreboding about Canadian women.

Some of those whom I succeeded in taking to bed were even more bizarre. A thirty-two-year-old librarian opened her limbs for me less than half an hour after we met at a party, and was proposing marriage within the hour. Then she gave me a lecture on my new responsibilities as her future husband. It was to be my duty to provide for her in comfort while I lived and after my death—that is, I had to take out a life insurance policy. In altogether less than two hours this strange creature was ready to marry me and bury me. She wouldn't leave until I explained to her that I came from a tribe which buried the widow alive beside her dead husband.

In those days I brooded a good deal about the arid relationship between the sexes, the distance which seemed to exist even between most married couples. I thought it had something to do with the fact that there were no bidets in the bathrooms. "If we had met here," I wrote to Paola, "you would have never let me get around you."

I spent a lot of time writing letters, mostly to my mother and Paola, and their replies were my best company.

My unpleasant if mercifully brief romances in Toronto were mere preludes to my encounter with Ann, a mercilessly irrational woman who had a profound influence on my life—as if to prove that the best way to teach a man is to make him suffer. We had two abortive affairs, with years in between which altered her personality a great deal, though her genius for the incongruous remained unaffected. I first met her at the Lake Couchiching Conference, which I attended that summer in order to get acquainted with some of my future colleagues at the university.

Couchiching is one of the thousands of lakes which make the unindustrialized regions of northern Ontario still wild and beautiful, in spite of the annual motorized invasion from the cities. On one large tract of shoreline, surrounded by dense woods, there is a YMCA camp which is turned over each summer to a ten-day conference on the great issues of the country and the world. From the shores of the Atlantic and the Pacific, three to four hundred Canadians converge on Couchiching: professors, newspapermen, high school teachers, television commentators, librarians, housewives active in community affairs, even a couple of odd politicians —in short, all kinds of people who *care*, and spend most of their lives indoors. Such summer conferences by water, trees and open sky are very popular among North American intellectuals, and justly so, for it's much more profitable to discuss the balance of terror, automation and the population explosion in shorts and the fresh air than in stiff suits and stuffy lecture halls. Besides, one is not obliged to attend every speech or discussion. It's possible to take a dip in the lake, lie on the dock in the sun, or just walk barefoot in the deliciously prickly grass. People who have to wear the burden of respectable common sense for eleven months of the year can spit on the ground, holler to hear their own voices and wait for the echo, scratch their bellies in public— while husbands and wives have the additional option of getting the stale air of the marital bedroom out of their lungs. Of course those who happen to have nothing better to do, assemble in the conference hall; but according to my personal calculations (which aren't necessarily accurate) about half a dozen adulteries are consummated during the discussion of one single aspect of a world crisis.

However, it would be misleading to claim extraordinary vitality and sophistication for Canada's intellectual community. I was billeted with five other bachelors, and there were several evenings when all five of them stayed in the cabin, drinking. They were all university graduates, two of them PhDs, and yet, while the woods and the lakeshore were filled with wandering girls and lonely wives, these supposedly intelligent, bright, healthy young men chose to sit on their bunks, holding on to a bottle for dear life and exchanging inane dirty jokes, as if they'd been locked in. I found the spectacle of these young people drinking away such marvellous opportunities absolutely incredible. When I left them to try my luck in the dark, they used to laugh at me and call me, with amiable contempt, 'the mad teetotaler'.

There was a newspaper man named Guy MacDonald at the conference, covering the discussions for one of the big dailies, though his regular job was writing nameless editorials. He was short, skinny and bowlegged, had thinning hair and a large sunburned nose, and wore old-fashioned wire-framed spectacles, which gave a kind of dignified unity to his plainness. Yet his wife was a pretty woman, the sort of blooming English beauty whose hair and skin combine the tints of blonde and redhead—all soft colours and contours, bursting with tensions. They had brought along their two daughters, who had unfortunately inherited their father's physique. The older girl told me she was 'nine and a half', so the MacDonalds must have been married for at least ten years, but Guy MacDonald was still anxious to please his wife, and always turned the conversation around to her when she was present. She used to listen to him with an expression which seemed to say *I'm smarter than my husband.* One morning, when we were sitting together on the edge of the dock, with our backs to the sun and our feet in the water, he told me that he had been born in Ottawa while Ann came from Victoria, British Columbia. The fact of their meeting and marrying in spite of the vast distance that separated them at birth struck him as strange and wonderful.

'You know,' he said, turning to pat his wife's knee, stretching out his arm with a long, slow gesture as if he was reaching across the thousands of miles, over the forests, the prairies, the lakes, the mountains, 'Ann comes from the West Coast—she grew up in Victoria.' Ann reacted to his remark and his touch with a martyred sigh—not crudely obvious, but perceptible.

'It isn't fair, but I can't forgive Guy that the girls inherited his looks,' she told me once when I found her alone on the dock keeping an eye on her daughters, who were splashing about in the water.

Late one night, as I was groping through the darkened camp on my way to meet a girl, I passed by the MacDonalds' cabin. Ann was sitting on the doorstep, and she called out like a sentry: 'Who goes there?'

'Hi! It's Andrew Vajda.'

'Where are you off to?'

It unnerves me to shout down the silence in the dark, so I walked over to her. 'I'm going to meet somebody.'

'Good for you,' she said resentfully. 'I'm not meeting anybody. The girls are asleep and Guy's playing bridge somewhere. I haven't a thing to do but sit here and count the stars.'

'You don't have to worry about the children in this place—

why don't you go and join him?'

'Why should I? I'm glad to be alone for a change.' Her voice was hostile, as if she wanted to be rid of me as well. Yet she added, in an urgent tremolo that sounded like a confession of availability, 'Why don't you sit down? We could watch the sky together.' I'd never known a woman whose moods changed so abruptly: she used to talk with drastically different intonations within the same sentence. Even on the dock, during the most casual conversation, Ann's voice would keep flapping about like a flag in contrary winds, as if her soul were in the grip of a savage storm.

No sooner had she tempted me to sit down beside her than she warned me off with heavy virtue. *'I don't invite men further than my doorstep,'* she said significantly, 'so don't you get ideas.'

'I'd be glad to keep you company, but I'm already late.'

'Oh well then . . . Help me up though, will you? I've been sitting here so long, my leg's gone to sleep.'

I raised Ann to her feet and she pulled me against her, placing my two hands firmly on her buttocks. I could feel them move through her flimsy summer skirt and I couldn't resist, even though I knew that there was a nice, bright girl waiting for me, with whom I would spend a far more pleasant evening than with this erratic housewife. It was a compulsive submission to the immediate sensation. As soon as the currents of our skins connected (in the darkness, filled with the faint but mesmerizing smell of the lake), I wanted Ann as desperately as if I'd never touched a woman in my life. I dragged her away from the cabin in search of a soft patch of grass protected by bushes, and at first she giggled delightedly behind me. Then she stopped short and began to pull in the opposite direction.

'Wait, Andy,' she said unhappily.

'Why, what's wrong?'

'I don't know . . . I guess it's just that I love my husband, in a way.'

'God forbid me to spoil a good marriage!' I said, quickly dropping her hand. Since my memorable night with that overheated virgin, Mici, I've been immune to teases.

'It isn't so much that I'm in love with him,' she added, even more unhappily, 'but you see I've never been unfaithful to him.'

'Then you shouldn't start now.'

'That's not the way you're supposed to talk,' she protested with genuine indignation. 'You're supposed to seduce me.'

'If you need convincing, believe me, it isn't worth it.'

'I thought you Europeans were supposed to be heroes in the war of the sexes!'

'I'm a pacifist.'

Thus we dissipated in talk whatever feelings we may have had, and she wouldn't lie down on the grass until we were bored and sick of each other. It was long agony for brief pleasure. I'd hardly entered her when we heard Guy MacDonald's voice in the distance.

'Ann—Ann? Are you around? Ann?'

I tried to go on, certain that he wouldn't find us, but Ann pushed me away with the strength of a tigress. She stood up, brushed off her skirt and blouse and turned towards me questioningly, and I took a leaf or two out of her hair. As she started off towards the path, walking with deliberate casualness, she called out in a calm voice: 'I'm coming. I just went for a walk.'

I waited until they'd disappeared inside their cabin, then ran, hoping that my date would still be waiting for me. She wasn't.

The next morning I went to the conference hall and heard two depressing speeches about the day when people wouldn't have to work for a living and could devote all their time to leisure activities. When I got back to our bachelor quarters after lunch, my companions received me with leering faces. Mrs. MacDonald had been looking for me.

'Now we know where you spend your evenings!' said the tall, effeminate lecturer in political science. 'She's very pretty.' After a dramatic pause, he added, 'She was so anxious to find you, I'd bet a bottle of Scotch that she's decided to leave her husband and shack up with you.'

They were still laughing at their own jokes when Ann walked past our cabin, apparently not for the first time, and turned her head towards the open doorway. I rushed out to lead her away. I'd taken for granted that our joyless coupling would be quickly forgotten by both of us and I couldn't imagine what she wanted from me. She was wearing a shapeless sack dress which didn't show her figure, and she looked grim, almost possessed. So it was unlikely that she wanted us to mend our broken romance.

'I must talk to you,' she announced. 'I have to talk to someone. I feel so guilty.'

'Oh, no!' I protested feebly. 'What on earth for?' We walked between the cabins, trying not to look too conspicuous.

'I'm thinking of telling Guy about it. He might be mad at me, but at least I'd get it off my conscience. I can't stand feeling guilty.'

'Are you religious?'

'No, of course not. I was raised as an Anglican, but I've grown out of it.'

'What's your problem then? You don't really care about Guy.'

'I just don't think it was right,' she said stubbornly.

'I see. You no longer believe in sin, but it bothers you just the same, out of force of habit.' I tried to be flippant, to prevent her from being overcome by the majesty of her tragic mood. It didn't work. Ann kept repeating that she felt guilty.

'Look, we didn't really make love. We'd hardly got started when your husband called.'

Ann brightened immediately. 'That's true!' she exclaimed. 'It isn't as though we got to the point of anything *serious*.' Her eyes began to shine with innocence; she wasn't pretty now, she was beautiful. Apparently what she was looking for wasn't redemption but qualification – a technical loophole, so to speak. 'You'd say we were just necking, really. Necking a little hard,' she added, and smiled at an elderly registrar passing by us.

I should have been relieved that she accepted my insincere white lie, but I was hurt. It was the first time a woman who'd made love with me thought that she hadn't – and actually looked glad about it!

'Guess I'll go for a swim,' she sang as she ran off. 'Bye-bye.'

Nor was this the end of it. Mrs MacDonald began to haunt me at parties, both at the camp and back in Toronto. Whenever the conversation got around to the affairs of those wives who were not present, she used to proclaim loudly and righteously: 'I've never slept with any man but my husband.' Then she turned to stare at me defiantly as if daring me to challenge her statement. It got so that everybody was convinced that we were having an affair, and even her husband began to eye me suspiciously.

To regain my peace of mind (and to avoid the real danger of an unpleasant scene with Guy MacDonald) I stopped going to places where Ann was likely to be present, but I began dreaming about her. Once I was in an aeroplane and suddenly Ann jumped up from her seat and cried out, her voice silencing the roar of the jet engines, 'I've never made love with anyone but my husband. Not *really*.' Then all the passengers got up and began to shake their fists at me. Another night, I was giving a lecture when she marched into the classroom, wearing her pink two-piece bathing suit from Couchiching, and shouted to my students: 'I want you to know that I never really made love with Professor Vajda!' I woke in sweats of embarrassment.

17 On More than Enough

Pleasure deprives a man of his faculties quite as much as pain.
Plato

I suppose seven years of lecturing made me susceptible to the notion that I had something to teach: there appears to be no other explanation for my indulging in these reminiscences with the idea of edifying the young. Still, I'm glad I've written them. They may offer little to the reader, but they've been rewarding for the author: I find it increasingly difficult to take myself seriously.

It seems now that whenever I thought I learned something about people or life in general, I was merely changing the form of my immutable ignorance – which is what compassionate philosophers call the nature of knowing. But to speak only of my search for happiness in love: apart from the time when I was at the mercy of teenage girls, I've never been so miserable with women as I was when I knew all the scores and had the prerequisites of a carefree bachelor life. When I came back from Lake Couchiching to Toronto, I moved into a modern apartment and furnished it with a huge bed, books, prints, a stereo system and one of the few bidets in North America. Later I even bought a sports car. I didn't have much cash, but my job at the university assured me of a good credit rating. In North America merchants consider corrupt politicians, civil servants and academics the best credit risks, because their jobs come with a nearly foolproof lifetime guarantee. I possessed average good looks and was also the right age: women are partial to men in their late twenties, especially if they have a Latin bathroom and are fond of women in every way.

I'd also grown quite adept at recognizing the women who weren't for me, and unpleasant surprises of the kind I described earlier occurred infrequently. Now I was unlucky with women who were both lovable and loving.

My trouble was that they were too numerous. I fell in love with them at the glint of an eye, at the sight of a well-rounded bosom (or a small, pointed one), at the sound of a husky voice or for less obvious reasons I was in too much of a hurry to analyse. Having a place of my own and irregular working hours, I could finally fulfil my boyhood fantasies and enjoy several love affairs concurrently.

The time was right – not only for me, but for my lovers as well. High living had become part of the atmosphere. When I arrived in Toronto, I could walk on the main avenues of the city on a Saturday evening without seeing a single soul except for a few drunks. As the straight rows of ugly boxes which passed for streets and the innumerable billboards and neon signs clearly testified, people seemed to be interested in little else than buying and selling the basic necessities. They spent their free time watching television in their underground recreation rooms, sitting around their backyard barbecues, or driving about in their new cars. They seemed to be afraid of getting too far away from the things they had so recently bought, and from the mates who had helped them to choose the house, the furniture, the car. It was a puritan world, but luckily I was able to get only a brief glimpse of it. People were getting used to their standard of living and suddenly became interested in life. Imaginative new buildings sprang up, whole streets of old houses were renovated and transformed into exotic boutiques, art galleries, bookshops and outdoor cafés, and on warm evenings so many people were strolling about that it sometimes took me a quarter of an hour to walk one block. The divorce rate soared, as did the number of riding clubs, women's committees for the support of the arts, Great Books discussion groups and other organizations which could provide an alibi for a wife when she felt like taking a lover. This was the phenomenon which became known as the North American Sexual Revolution, and I was bent on making the most of it.

The result was like driving in a speeding car through a beautiful landscape: I had an impression of all the exciting hills and valleys, contours and colours, but I was moving too fast to be able to take a good look. I often regretted not being able to know my lovers better – though I had to take considerable pains to prevent them from knowing me too well. Women have the habit of leaving a nightgown, a makeup case, a pair of nylons, at their boy friend's apartment; steadfast Scottish-Canadian girls even left their diaphragms with me. Hiding the belongings of one from the eyes of another was difficult and nerve-racking – along with the problems of timing, confusion of identities and constant lying. Nor was I always successful: there were the inevitable slips and scenes. Once I was caught by failing to explain successfully why I had put a diaphragm in an old shoe box, under a pile of laundry. I'd remembered to hide the thing all right, but had forgotten to put it back in the bathroom cabinet before its owner's next visit. I became jumpy and listless, a physical and mental wreck, unable to have a good time, let alone be happy. Yet I couldn't stop. After all, wasn't I lucky, being able to go to bed with nearly all the women I wanted? I used to envy myself, in the pit of my misery. More and more, I found myself drawn to women who were themselves getting battered by life.

That's how I got together with Ann MacDonald again. I hadn't met her for about a year, when one afternoon I saw her sitting a few tables away from me in a newly opened Hungarian coffee house. We smiled and waved and when she was leaving, she stopped by me.

'How are you?'

'How are you?'

Neither of us knew what to say next. I asked her to sit down and have another espresso with me, if she wasn't in a hurry.

'I'd love to,' she said in a strained voice, 'I have a lot of time on my hands these days.' It was late November and she was wearing a black velvet dress which set off perfectly her rounded figure and bright rosy complexion. 'I like this Hungarian place,' she remarked as she sat down, 'it's wonderful to have places like these in stuffy old Toronto.' For a while we discussed the changes European immigrants were bringing to the city and of course I took full credit for them.

'I'm sorry,' she finally said, 'that we had so little time to get to know each other at Couchiching.'

'I thought even the time we had was too much for you.'

'Yes, you must think I behaved like an idiot. As it turned out, Guy couldn't care less what I do.'

'Why? What happened?'

'Oh, it's a long story. Now he claims that I make him feel old and unattractive. So he seduces his secretaries. I wouldn't mind so much, but he insists on telling me all the details. I get the impression he's expecting me to applaud him.'

It's because you always tried to look smarter, I thought. 'Oh well, that means your opinion is still the most important thing for him. It means he still loves you.'

'I doubt it. But I don't really worry about my marriage any more. I made up my mind to enjoy life.'

She threw promising glances at me, but I had a date, and I wasn't going to miss it this time. We talked some more, about the weather and Toronto, and parted amicably. Old enemies, new friends.

In the following months, I heard many stories about Ann MacDonald's love affairs. Sometimes she told me about them herself, at our accidental meetings. There was a new sensuous evenness to her personality; she had the melancholy self-assurance of a woman who has several lovers to look after. As we exchanged confidences, I told her about my problem of wanting too many women.

'I know how it is,' she sighed. 'I'm the same way myself.'

'You're the one I really need. You understand me – with you I wouldn't have to pretend.'

'It'd be nice,' she conceded wistfully, reaching out to press my hand. 'But let's be practical, Andy – we'd only compound each other's problems.'

She expressed her refusal with such affectionate regret that only later did I realize that she had turned me down. The disaffected housewife had become a lady of the world, and I couldn't help being impressed. I began thinking about her, wishing she would ring me up, wondering jealously about the men in her stories. Did she talk to me for the same reason that her husband told her about his exploits? Was she trying to annoy me or did she just want an audience? Gradually I became convinced, not without misgivings, that I was in love with her.

Thereafter, I tried to seduce Ann MacDonald each time we met, but I didn't succeed until the winter of 1962. I cornered her at a pary, while her husband was busy in another room and none of her lovers seemed to be around. She was wearing a low-cut evening gown, and I literally backed her into a corner and leaned so hard against her that I could feel the warmth of her breasts through my dinner jacket.

'I got the worst of you,' I protested. 'Here you are, a wise and beautiful woman, and I have to content myself with memories of a silly bitch at Lake Couchiching. It isn't fair. We must put this right. Besides, I think I'm in love with you.'

Ann's eyes gleamed with something more like a flash of lightning than my old familiar glint, but her voice was motherly and soothing. 'You're a stubborn boy, aren't you?'

'I don't mind being a boy. In fact, the older I get, the less I mind being a boy. I want to rest my head on your breasts.'

'You're a dear-dear baby.'

That I didn't like, baby was too young. I let her drift away.

After midnight, when the guests no longer bothered hiding in dark corners for their furtive but passionate embraces and we were all heady from having too much of too little, I went in search of Ann again. Discovering her in the hands of our tall and lecherous host, I waited by stubbornly until the appearance of our jealous hostess.

Then Ann was glad to notice me. 'I don't know where Guy is,' she said, flushed. 'If you've nothing better to do, you can drive me home.'

By the time we reached the street, she'd agreed to drop in at my place. She filled my small car with her scent and gently stroked the back of my neck as we drove along in silence. I was exalted and relaxed, dreaming of our happy future. There'd be no more running for either of us, I'd be Ann's slave and spend with her every moment she could spare from her husband and children.

Ann's thoughts must have been different, for she suddenly withdrew her hand from my neck. 'Listen,' she said anxiously, prompted perhaps by the memory of an unpleasant experience, 'I don't know enough about you, we never really made love, you know. I hope you aren't one of those men who slip in and out just like that.' The very thought made her belligerent. 'Frankly I have enough lovers right now and I don't need little skirmishes, even for old times' sake. If you want anything you have to promise me performance.'

I wonder how other accidents happen. I shot through a red light and ran up on the sidewalk, stopping the car just short of a lamp post. 'Listen,' she said fiercely, 'if you get me into an accident and my daughters hear about us I'm going to kill you. Can't you drive?'

It was about one in the morning and we were on a quiet residential street. No one had seen us. I backed the car carefully off the sidewalk and for a moment thought of turning it around and driving her back to the party. But the idea of having unfinished business with the same woman twice was intolerable. 'Don't worry,' I seethed, 'you'll have a night you'll never forget.'

Neither of us said another word until we were inside my apartment. 'I'm sorry,' Ann pouted as I helped her off with her coat, 'I didn't mean to upset you. It's just that a woman is always at such a disadvantage. She never knows what she's agreeing to.'

'As a matter of fact, I was planning to make you fall in love with me,' I said sourly.

'Well, it's still not too late.' She leaned against me and placed my hands on her buttocks, just as before. 'And we don't have to lie on a scraggly patch of grass in the woods,' she reminded me, and slowly rotated her buttocks to please my hands. I tried to undress her, but she didn't want help. If Ann demanded performance, she was also willing to give it, and she did a strip-tease for me, throwing her clothes away with a tempting grace of anticipation.

Yet, when I tried to move above her on the bed, she held me away. 'I don't like it from above,' she said with thinly veiled exasperation. 'Do it sideways, please.'

I grew dead in an instant. Playing for time, I began fondling her.

After a few desperate tries, Ann conceded our defeat. 'Never mind, I've lost my impetus too, so you don't have to worry. We just don't have much luck with each other, I guess.' She leaped out of bed and collected her things, letting go of her temper on her bra, which seemed to have disappeared. I finally spotted it beneath the bed and crawled under to retrieve it for her.

'Thanks,' Ann said, 'you're wonderful!'

She withdrew to the bathroom with her clothes and handbag. I didn't plan to follow her but after about twenty minutes I went to see if she was all right. I found her fully dressed, elegant and composed, brushing her eyelashes. When she saw the reflection of my guilty face in the mirror, she smiled at me with affectionate indifference. Then she took a final, thoughtful look at herself.

'Oh, well,' she concluded, 'one orgasm more or less doesn't really matter, does it?'

The truth and humiliation of that moment marked, I believe, the belated end of my youth. I wanted to go to a new country. To some peaceful faraway place. A few days later when I heard about an opening in the Department of Philosophy at The University of Michigan I applied for the job. Ann Arbor didn't turn out to be as quiet as I had thought, nor was I quite ready yet to sit down and grow old. But the adventures of a middle-aged man are another story.

Praise for *An Innocent Millionaire*

"Vizinczey is one of the great writers in the English language today."
—Juan Angel Juristo, *El Independiente* (Madrid)

"A dazzling performance. It is as if Balzac had come back to life and written a novel about the modern world of jet planes and chemical manufacturers."
—Robert Fulford, *Toronto Star*

"To say that this amazing novel is about a young man who finds fabulous treasure, only to be systematically robbed of it, is like saying that *Hamlet* is about a mad prince wandering round a castle."
—Harry Reid, *Glasgow Herald*

"Balzac on a treasure hunt. With cunning simplicity Vizinczey confronts the highest and lowest concerns of humanity. He tells foreground stories of everyday life while all the time he has in mind the divine and the diabolical, the abject and the sublime. The novel is constructed with supreme dramatic skill and it has total inner coherence."
—Hans Romer, *Nürnberger Zeitung* (Nuremberg)

"Powerfully persuasive fiction, filled with human insight, literary poise, high imagination and, best of all, pure comedy . . . Vizinczey has placed himself in a category with Conrad and Nabokov as a foreigner who handles English in a way that strikes jealousy into the heart of the native English-speaker."
—Leslie Hanscom, *Newsday*

"A masterpiece of living, thrilling and subtle narrative art. Vizinczey holds a mirror up to our world and to each one of us, and hardly anyone will be able to look into it without being frightened—but at the same time inspired to live differentiy and to better purpose."
—Peter Ebner, *Die Furche* (Vienna)

"It's gigantic. It's full of the insights and obsessions of a man who has lived an extraordinary life and observed, with a filing-cabinet eye, the corruption of the powerful and the foibles of the insignificant. . . . Charming and very, very tough."
—Peter Carvosso, *Evening Herald* (Dublin)

"A great novel. Vizinczey sets in motion a multitude of extraordinarily alive characters, good and bad, and he astounds us with a *Comédie humaine* of the modern world."
—Eva Haldimann, *Neue Zürcher Zeitung* (Zurich)

"Superb, unpredictable pacing. . . . An anatomy of the ways of the world rivaling Balzac's *Lost Illusions*. . . . A contemporary version of Stendhal on love and Balzac on money."
—Michael Stern, *San Jose Mercury News*

Praise for *Truth and Lies in Literature*

"What is most impressive about these essays (apart from their range and erudition) is the way that literature and life are so subtly intertwined with each other. Mr. Vizinczey unerringly knows how to find the weight of experience, and states it in unflinching, aphoristic English."
—Mark Le Fanu, *The Times* (London)

"A challenge to any form of half-heartedness and all kinds of resignation and timidity. Vizinczey's view of literature pushes the literary center back to what is meaningful and alive, away from all academic spinelessness and easy formalism."
—Christer Enander, *Kvällsposten* (Stockholm)

"An argument in favor of lucidity, liberty and the enjoyment of life; an exposé of stupidity, deceit and literary squalor. Stimulating in his love as in his hates. Vizinczey's hypercritical and plain-spoken writing will undoubtedly help more than one reader (and more than one writer) to be less pedantic and pretentious, to become wiser and more lucid, and also, perhaps, more courageous. . . . An intellectually exciting and morally inspiring book."
—Jesus Moreno Sanz, *Diario 16* (Madrid)